BETTER NOT CRY

A REBEKKA FRANCK NOVEL

WILLOW ROSE

BUOY MEDIA LLC

BOOKS BY THE AUTHOR

MYSTERY/HORROR NOVELS

- In One Fell Swoop
- Umbrella Man
- Blackbird Fly
- To Hell in a Handbasket
- Edwina

7TH STREET CREW SERIES

- What Hurts the Most
- You Can Run
- You Can't Hide
- Careful Little Eyes

EMMA FROST SERIES

- Itsy Bitsy Spider
- Miss Dolly had a Dolly
- Run, Run as Fast as You Can
- Cross Your Heart and Hope to Die

- Peek-a-Boo I See You
- Tweedledum and Tweedledee
- Easy as One, Two, Three
- There's No Place like Home
- Slenderman
- Where the Wild Roses Grow

JACK RYDER SERIES

- Hit the Road Jack
- Slip out the Back Jack
- The House that Jack Built
- Black Jack

REBEKKA FRANCK SERIES

- One, Two...He is Coming for You
- Three, Four...Better Lock Your Door
- Five, Six...Grab your Crucifix
- Seven, Eight...Gonna Stay up Late
- Nine, Ten...Never Sleep Again
- Eleven, Twelve...Dig and Delve
- Thirteen, Fourteen...Little Boy Unseen
- Better Not Cry

HORROR SHORT-STORIES

- Mommy Dearest
- The Bird
- Better watch out
- Eenie, Meenie
- Rock-a-Bye Baby
- Nibble, Nibble, Crunch
- Humpty Dumpty
- Chain Letter

SCIENCE FICTION/PARANORMAL SUSPENSE/FANTASY NOVELS

SCIENCE FICTION

- The Surge
- Girl Divided

AFTERLIFE SERIES

- Beyond
- Serenity
- Endurance
- Courageous

THE WOLFBOY CHRONICLES

- A Gypsy Song
- I am WOLF

DAUGHTERS OF THE JAGUAR

- Savage
- Broken

Copyright Willow Rose 2017
Published by BUOY MEDIA LLC
All rights reserved.

No part of this book may be reproduced, scanned, or distributed in any printed or electronic form without permission from the author.

This is a work of fiction. Any resemblance of characters to actual persons, living or dead is purely coincidental. The Author holds exclusive rights to this work. Unauthorized duplication is prohibited.

Cover design by Juan Villar Padron,
https://juanjjpadron.wixsite.com/juanpadron

Special thanks to my editor Janell Parque
http://janellparque.blogspot.com/

To be the first to hear about new releases and bargains—from Willow Rose—sign up below to be on the VIP List. (I promise not to share your email with anyone else, and I won't clutter your inbox.)

- SIGN UP TO BE ON THE VIP LIST HERE :
http://eepurl.com/wcGej

Follow Willow Rose on BookBub:
https://www.bookbub.com/authors/willow-rose

Connect with Willow Rose:

willow-rose.net

*Santa baby, slip a sable under the tree
   for me
Been an awful good girl
Santa baby, and hurry down the chimney
   tonight*

— EARTHA KITT, "Santa Baby"

*You better watch out
You better not cry
Better not pout
I'm telling you why
Santa Claus is coming to town*

— HAVEN GILLESPIE, "Santa Claus is Coming to Town."

1

For six-year-old Tobin, it all started...and ended... with a plate of cookies and a glass of milk. It was only the beginning of December, yet Tobin insisted on putting out the cookies and milk for Santa on December 1st and every day from then on. Just in case, he told his parents. Just in case Santa decided to be early this year.

They had barely finished Thanksgiving dinner before he pulled out his stocking from the big box of Christmas stuff and hung it by the fireplace, ready for Santa to fill it up.

Tobin's mother, Jacqueline, enjoyed her son's excitement around Christmas, as she herself was a big fan of this particular holiday and always had been. Jacqueline, or Jackie, as most people called her, encouraged her son to put out the cookies and milk. And this year, Tobin was especially excited since he had made a big wish for Santa. His only worry was that this was one he wouldn't be able to fit into his stocking. It was one Tobin believed Santa might not even be able to fit into that big bag of his. It was a wish so big, Tobin had written a letter to Santa already in the middle of November to make sure the old bearded man with the jolly laugh had enough time to find the right one, the one with the big brown eyes looking back at him from the cage in the Animal Adoption Center at the mall. The little white pit bull puppy with the black spots on his back and paws so big they almost looked like clown's feet.

He had named it Rocky.

His mom and dad had told him it would be difficult for Santa to fit Rocky inside his bag, but Santa would just have to work a little harder on that Christmas magic of his, Tobin thought. If anyone could do it, it was Santa. Tobin believed he could and he would.

That was why he put out the cookies and milk starting on the first day of December. Just in case Santa had to be early to get Rocky to Tobin. Just in case. Besides, Santa deserved a little extra this year if he was going to give Tobin such a big present.

Tobin placed the plate of freshly baked cookies by the fireplace before bedtime, and the glass of milk next to it. His hands almost shivered with excitement and Jackie worried her son wouldn't be able to sleep much. She leaned over and kissed him on his head.

"Don't be disappointed if Santa doesn't come tonight," Jackie said. "There are many nights before Christmas."

"I know," Tobin said with a shrug. "It's just in case he does stop by a little early."

"All right, then," Jackie said and kissed him again. He looked so cute in those little pajamas of his with all the planes on them. She smelled his newly washed hair. She remembered when Alyssa used to smell like that. Jackie glanced toward the staircase. She didn't often see her teenage daughter anymore. Not because she wasn't home. She was up there in her room on the computer or phone most of the time. She just never wanted to hang out with her family anymore. Jackie could never really figure out what she did on that computer up there and had given up controlling it a long time ago. She just wished her daughter would get outside and get some fresh air occasionally and not stay cooped up in her room, getting paler and paler as the days passed. She used to be such a healthy kid, always in the pool or out surfing with her friends. But not anymore. Jackie couldn't understand why she didn't want to go outside more often. This was Florida. December was a great time to be outside, often the best time of the year.

"You think there are enough cookies, Mommy?" Tobin said, concerned.

Jackie chuckled. "I think Santa will be very happy. Now, off to bed. You know Santa doesn't come till you're sound asleep, right?"

Tobin's face lit up. He sprang for the stairs. "Come on, Mommy. I have to go to bed now. Hurry."

Jackie smiled and walked toward the stairs. "I'm coming, I'm coming."

She glanced back at the milk and cookies before following her son up the stairs, wondering, hoping, and praying that Tobin wouldn't cry the next morning when he realized Santa hadn't been there yet. Otherwise, it might end up being a very long December. Very long indeed.

2

"Santa is the best, Mommy. I love Santa."

Tobin yawned as he spoke. He was under the covers all tucked in and Jackie had finished reading a story. His eyelids were half closed already.

"I know you do," Jackie said.

She looked at the clock on the nightstand. It was eight o'clock and Steve hadn't come home yet. She sighed and felt a pinch in her stomach. The renovation company worked him so hard, especially at this time of year. They had barely finished hurricane season with all the extra debris they had to get rid of and this year it was worse than it had been in years since Irma had rushed through the entire state. Cocoa Beach hadn't been hit too badly, but there was still a lot to clean up and the company was running behind.

Now, Steve didn't pick up the garbage himself. He was in an administrative position and that was why he often had to work late. Tonight, he hadn't even called home to tell her he'd be late. It bothered her and she was worried about him, especially since he didn't seem to enjoy his work very much. He was often miserable once he got home and would hardly speak to any of them except with grunts and grumbles.

"But now you have to sleep."

Jackie kissed Tobin one last time, then turned out the lights, except for the one in the walk-in closet that Tobin wanted on as nightlight since he was terrified of the darkness.

"Do you think he'll come tonight?" Tobin asked as she approached the door and had her hand on the handle.

She sighed. She knew he wouldn't be there tonight. Of course, Santa wouldn't come on December 1st, but the boy was so hopeful, it was hard to crush such sincere hope. Fact was, Jackie and Steve had already bought the puppy for Tobin and the Adoption Center would keep it till they could give it to him on Christmas morning. But she could hardly tell him that, could she? It would ruin the surprise and since he so sincerely believed it was Santa who brought the presents, she could hardly let herself destroy that. It would come out at some point and ruin all the magic of Christmas. She remembered the day Alyssa came home from school and told her mother that none of the other kids believed in Santa anymore and so now she didn't either.

"You gotta believe in Santa," Jackie had told her.

Secretly, she suspected that Alyssa still believed but just didn't dare to say it. Jackie once believed she had seen him. Jackie chuckled at the memory when walking out of Tobin's room and approaching Alyssa's door. It was covered in signs telling everyone to stay out, to knock before entering.

She couldn't have been much more than five or six when it happened. It wasn't on Christmas Eve when most people usually saw him. It was in the middle of December when she had heard the rustling from downstairs and hurried down. She had spotted Santa in her living room, sitting in her dad's recliner. As he saw her, he tapped his lap and signaled for her to come and sit on it and so she had. He had laughed his deep laugh while asking her what she wanted for Christmas and Jackie had told him, whispering how she wished for a new bike, a Barbie doll with purple nails and...oh, yes...for her parents to no longer be divorced.

Santa had laughed, holding his stomach, then told her he couldn't give her all of that, but he could give her something else.

"What?" she had asked, looking up into his red glowing eyes that looked like two beautiful Christmas globes.

Santa had turned his lips upward in a grin when suddenly the light was turned on in the living room and her mom had spoken with a sleepy voice.

"What's going on down here?"

Jackie looked up at her, then said: "It's Santa, Mommy. He wants to know what I want for Christmas."

"What are you talking about, Jackie? It's not even Christmas yet."

Jackie had then turned her head back to look at

Santa, but he was gone and she was sitting in the recliner all alone.

"Get back to bed," her mother had said angrily. "I don't like you running around at nighttime."

"But...?"

"Go to bed."

Today, Jackie knew it had just been a dream. Just a product of a child's vivid imagination. She had probably just been sleepwalking, as she had been known to do before. Jackie shook her head again when thinking about how determined she had been in convincing her mother and brother the next day that Santa had actually been there at her house. She had waited for him to come back, but of course, he never did. And her mother had gotten so sick of hearing about it, she had finally told Jackie that there was no Santa. He didn't exist. It had broken Jackie's heart and, just like that, POOF, the magic of Christmas was gone.

Jackie knocked on Alyssa's door and waited for her to yell.

"What?"

Jackie peeked inside. As usual, Alyssa was sitting on her bed, her laptop on top of it, headset on, and speaking into her microphone.

"Wait a sec, my mom's here," she told whomever she was chatting with.

Jackie often worried it was some pedophile guy from Russia who took pictures of her, or maybe a member of some gang that stole young girls and trafficked them. But Alyssa usually just rolled her eyes at her when she addressed it and told her she wasn't stupid, and then slammed the door.

"What?" Alyssa asked and pulled one side of the headphones from her ear to hear what her mother said.

"Your brother is sleeping. You have one more hour until bedtime."

Again, the rolling of the eyes, followed by a growl. "Mom, I know that. You don't have to come in here and tell me that."

"Just making sure you're still alive," Jackie said.

"Well, I am. Now, can you leave?"

"Who are you playing with?" Jackie asked.

Alyssa sighed, annoyed. "Chris, all right?"

"Who's Chris?"

"He's my friend."

"I've just never heard his name before."

"Well, now you have. Okay? Don't forget to close the door when you leave."

Alyssa put her headset back on, so she could no longer hear if Jackie said anything else. Jackie sighed and closed the door, trying hard to remember when Alyssa was younger. It was getting harder and harder to remember how cute she used to be.

3

Tobin woke up just as the clock struck midnight. Eyes wide open, he stared at the ceiling. Had he heard something? Was it a sound coming from the living room? Was someone down there? Could it be?

Santa!

Tobin leaped out of his bed, then stopped for a second and stared at the light coming from the closet. It had always scared him to pass it at night since he often imagined it being a gateway to another universe filled with monsters and that the portal might suck him into it like a spaceship into a black hole.

Tobin stared at the light coming from the closet, his breathing getting heavier while imagining the door slamming open, and almost feeling the suction from it.

Then he shook his head and looked away. No, he had more important things to do. If Santa was, in fact, downstairs bringing him Rocky, there was no time to waste.

Tobin opened the door and went into the hallway,

BETTER NOT CRY

bursting with excitement as he heard another noise come from the living room. It sounded like bells. And not just ordinary bells.

Santa. It has got to be Santa!

Tobin imagined Santa eating his cookies and drinking the milk while rubbing his belly and chuckling joyfully. He imagined his red cheeks getting redder from smiling so much and his beard being all white and fluffy as cotton candy.

But when Tobin reached the top of the stairs and looked down, he couldn't see anything. It was dark, but light emerged from the streetlamps outside and lit up the living room just enough for him to see that there was no Santa, there was no Rocky, and the cookies and milk were still where he had left them.

Disappointed, Tobin sulked. He was about to turn around and walk back to his room when he heard another sound. Excited once again, he looked down and saw ashes falling in clusters from inside the chimney.

It is him. It is Santa!

Tobin let out a small shriek and hurried down the stairs, closer to the chimney. A small cloud of ashes fell and filled the air. Tobin had told his mother to get the chimney cleaned for Santa, but she insisted he was used to it, that a little ash stuck inside of it wouldn't bother him much. As a matter of fact, it helped him slide down easier, she had said. But Tobin knew his mother was just saying that because she didn't want to spend money on getting the chimney cleaned. Christmas was expensive enough as it was.

Poor Santa. Struggling to get down.

Tobin stood for a little while by the fireplace, watching the ashes fall down, coughing whenever some of it hit his face, worrying that Santa might get stuck or maybe even sick.

Nonsense. Santa does this all the time.

Tobin could hardly keep the excitement inside. He was about to explode while waiting, imagining Santa handing him Rocky and how he was going to play with the dog all night and never go back to bed.

I am gonna kiss him and hug him and play fetch and...and...

Tobin stared at the chimney as the movement inside of it stopped. No more ashes fell, no more sounds came from inside of it.

"Santa?" Tobin said with a small shriek.

He dropped to his knees and peeked inside. It was pitch dark in the chimney. A lump of ashes fell on his face and he spurted and coughed and pulled his head away, then wiped it off. He waited a few seconds more for Santa to come down, but still, nothing happened. Once again, Tobin peeked up into the chimney to see if Santa might be stuck further up. He couldn't see Santa, but he could see a set of red glowing Christmas globes.

"Santa?" he said again.

There was something about the eyes that made him back away, and that was when a voice from inside the chimney, said:

"Hello, Tobin."

"Santa?" Tobin answered cautiously. "Is...is th-th-that you?"

The laughter rumbled inside the chimney. That very distinctive yet familiar laugh that could only come from one particular person.

"Ho-Ho-Ho."

Tobin's face lit up. It *was* him, he was really here inside Tobin's chimney. But why wasn't he coming down? Why wasn't he already in the living room, eating cookies and drinking milk? Was he stuck in the chimney and couldn't get down? Was he hurt? Had he brought Rocky?

"It *is* you, Santa."

Tobin dropped to his knees again, crawled closer this time, and peeked inside again. The red glowing Christmas globes stared back at him. They were sparkling in the darkness. Tobin smiled.

"Did you bring Rocky?"

"I sure did," Santa said, his voice as deep as thunder. "Why don't you come a little closer, so you can see him?"

Tobin did as he was told and stuck most of his head into the chimney.

"A little closer," Santa said.

Tobin crawled. His fingers were getting black from soot.

"A little more, just a little bit and you're there."

"It's awfully dark in here, Santa," Tobin complained.

It made Santa laugh his hearty, deep, merry laughter. It seemed to make the entire chimney shake.

"Ho-ho-ho."

Tobin smiled and crept closer still, soot on his face

and arms and on his new pajamas that his mother was so fond of. It didn't matter, he thought to himself since soon he would have his puppy; soon, Rocky would be with him, and the pajamas could be washed and so could he.

"Reach out your hands, Tobin," Santa said and Tobin did as he was told, thinking only of Rocky and all the hours they were going to play together. "Both of them."

Tobin stretched his arms up and felt Santa's hands grab him, his long thin fingernails piercing into his skin. Tobin didn't even manage to scream. He was pulled up into the horrifying darkness and never saw daylight again. And worst of all, he never got to play with Rocky.

4

Jackie felt exhausted when she woke up the next morning. Even more than usual. She lifted her head from her pillow and glanced at Steve, then felt heavy. He had come home at ten the night before and smelled like perfume and alcohol. She had smelled it when kissing him and it had struck her right at that moment for the first time.

Steve was cheating on her.

That was why he had all those extra hours at work. That was why he always came home late at night making all sorts of excuses, grumbling and growling at all of them. It wasn't because of Irma, nor was it because he hated his job. It was because he didn't like being here with them at the house. He would much rather be somewhere else with that other woman.

Jackie had thought it through and it all made perfect sense. What she hadn't done was ask him or confront him with her speculations. Because what if they were just that? What if they were nothing but a product of her imagination? What if Steve had just hugged his secretary or someone else at work before coming home? What if they had grabbed a beer before going home at the end of a long day? Because they deserved it for working so long and hard?

It was possible, wasn't it?

Jackie sighed. She knew she was only fooling herself. She had watched enough soaps to know that if it looked like a duck, then it probably was one. And this was definitely a duck.

She got up and out of bed when Steve opened his eyes. She took a shower, ignoring him chirping *Good-morning* from the bed. With her eyes closed, letting the water bathe her, she wondered how she was going to approach this suspicion of hers. How did you do something like this? She and Steve had always been the perfect couple. Everyone had believed them to be the ones who would make it. *If anyone could*, they always said.

She shut off the water and dried herself, then walked back into the bedroom, still not uttering a word to him.

"Good morning," he said again while she disappeared into the walk-in closet and picked out her outfit for the day. She was going with jeans and the red top. She looked at herself in the mirror and realized she always wore the same thing, only the top changed color every day. She had five pairs of the same jeans and the same top in eight different colors.

Jackie sighed and discovered a pimple on her face,

right in the middle of her forehead. Wasn't she supposed to have stopped getting pimples now that she had turned forty? She had already started to get wrinkles. The most merciful thing would be for the pimples to at least stop. Was the world really this cruel?

Jackie sighed and left her reflection alone. Steve had gotten out of bed and was in the shower as she put on a little light makeup, something she usually didn't do anymore since she barely ever looked at herself in the mirror and Steve wasn't home anyway, so what was the use. But today, she put on mascara and eyeliner and a little lip-gloss. She thought it would make her feel better, but it didn't.

When Steve came out of the shower, Jackie disappeared into the hallway, avoiding him. She walked to Tobin's room and peeked inside. She was so excited to give him the puppy she could hardly contain it. She imagined Rocky would sleep in Tobin's room all night and help her wake him up in the mornings.

Tobin wasn't in his bed, but that wasn't unusual. Often, he got up before they did and was already in the living room watching TV till breakfast was ready. Alyssa, on the other hand, was impossible to get out of her bed. Jackie had a feeling she might be awake late at night, gaming with her online friends and not telling anyone. Jackie worried about her sleep and whether she got enough, but as long as you couldn't tell by her grades, she really had nothing to complain about. And she couldn't. Alyssa did very well in school.

Jackie knocked on her door, then opened it and

turned on the lights. Alyssa grumbled loudly from under the covers.

"Turn it off."

"Time to get up," Jackie said.

"I don't want to," Alyssa said.

"You have to. You have school today."

"I don't want to go to school."

"But you have to, sweetie."

"I hate school. It's so boring," she said.

It was true. School was too easy for Alyssa and always had been. Even though they had put her in the gifted programs in elementary school, it still hadn't challenged her enough. Alyssa had been so bored she often got herself into trouble in class. It had been a fight back then and still was to just get her to go.

"I hate this day," Alyssa said. "I hate this day, I hate school, and I hate you."

"That's not very nice to say," Jackie said. She was used to it, though. Alyssa was always so grumpy in the mornings and it wasn't unusual for her to tell her mother how much she hated her.

"I don't care," Alyssa said.

"All right. I'll make some breakfast. Get ready, okay?"

Alyssa answered with another grumble and Jackie left her. She walked toward the stairs, then wondered why the TV wasn't blasting like it usually was when Tobin had woken up earlier than the rest of them.

Why aren't the lights turned on?

"Tobin?"

She walked down the stairs, and then realized something very strange. Someone had lit the fireplace. They usually never used it since it was so warm in Florida. Only a few times a year when the temperature dropped below sixty-eight, they would put firewood in it and light it. Mostly for the fun of it and sometimes the kids would roast marshmallows. But it wasn't cold outside at all. Had Steve lit it? Had Tobin? No way. Tobin was the one who wanted the chimney to stay clean and cold for Santa to slide down.

The fire crackled as the wood burned in it. Jackie stared at it for a little while, then decided it was probably Steve who had turned it on, maybe to celebrate that it would be Christmas soon. He never thought Florida was quite Christmassy enough down here in the heat. Not like New York where he was from.

Jackie shrugged and walked into the kitchen, then pulled out the cereal when a smell filled her nostrils that made her want to throw up. As a former bookkeeper at the Brevard County Funeral Home & Crematory, she knew exactly what it was.

The smell of burned flesh.

PART I

5

The humid air wrapped me like a blanket. A nice warm blanket of air. Coming as I was from the cold winter in Denmark, it felt soothing on my dry skin. We had just landed in Orlando airport after ten hours in the air. We had then waited for an hour and a half to go through Customs, waited forever to get our luggage, and finally, finally, we had stepped outside the airport and could smell the air.

I pushed Sune in the wheelchair, almost envying him that he could just sit there for the entire trip. But then again, I think he would do anything to switch places with me.

Two years he had been in this chair, two tough years for all of us.

"Where do we go now, Mom?" Julie asked, dragging her own suitcase behind her.

Only just turned eleven years old, she was suddenly so grown up. So was Sune's son, Tobias, who was the same age. Sune's accident had done that to them. Forced them to grow up. I had asked for more help around the house, especially with William, who was now four years old and quite the handful. He was sitting in Sune's lap, giggling as I rolled them out to the curb.

"There's supposed to be a shuttle here somewhere that can take us to the car rental," I said, sweat already springing from my forehead. I was wearing way too many clothes for Florida. It was so hard when I stood in Denmark in forty-one-degree-weather and had to pack a suitcase for eighty-five degrees. It was just impossible to imagine it could feel this warm and humid in December.

"Mickey!" William exclaimed and pointed happily at a big sign for Disney's many parks. It was part of the deal with all three kids to go to the Magic Kingdom. We had saved for this trip for a very long time, so we were all determined to make the best of it.

But it wasn't just for pure pleasure. We were going to stay here for the entire month. I had been trying for almost a year to get a certain doctor to look at Sune, one with a specialty in this type of case. It was the last straw for us, the last hope we had to cling to. It was Sune who had found this guy and his clinic located about an hour outside of Orlando. He had been researching online after the doctors in Denmark had told us there wasn't any more they could do for him. He was never going to walk again. For two years, we had been running from one doctor to another. We had gone through each and every training program there was and he even had injections with Botox, which had been proven to help people who were paralyzed after a stroke. All to get Sune to walk again. But nothing had helped. Still, Sune refused to give up. He knew he was going to walk again. He was so determined, I even refused to give up. Somehow, he clung to that conviction so tightly. It was quite incredible for a man in his situation. Plus, he said, he had promised Tobias that he would walk again and Sune wasn't one to ever break a promise. Especially not to his son.

The doctor had agreed to see us two days after we landed, so we decided to make a trip out of it and celebrate Christmas in Florida among gators, mice speaking with high-pitched voices, and roller coasters. I, for one, hoped we would have time for some beach as well. Just a day or two lying in the white sand, listening to the waves would be like therapy for me after the last couple of years I had had. Between taking care of Sune, my job, William, and my dad, there was very little time for myself anymore. I was worn down and Sune knew it. He could see it on my face. My boss, Jens-Ole, knew it too and gave me the entire month off. To get back on track, he said.

"Over there," I said and pointed at the shuttle bus. I waved at the driver standing in front of it and he rushed to help us with our luggage.

6

It was a beautiful drive. Once we managed to get to our car and get Sune in the passenger seat, his wheelchair in the back, and all the rest of us and our luggage inside, we were ready for the next part of our little adventure. We used my phone and Google Maps to direct us toward Cocoa Beach, where I had rented a house that could fit all of us for the entire month. A house directly on the beach. It was very expensive, but I had been a little selfish, thinking if we stayed directly on the beach, there would be a chance for me to actually get to go to the beach and maybe even into the ocean once or twice. I knew we were mostly here for Sune's appointment with this doctor, who had an extremely high success rate, and for the kids to visit the parks, but there was no reason why I couldn't enjoy myself as well, was there?

I had asked my dad to come with us on the trip, but the ten-hour flight was too much for him, he said. He was too old for that now. As I drove on 520 beach-line and crossed the bridges leading to the islands, I started to think it was for the best. I hated to leave him back at the house all alone, but it was good for us to just be the five of us. To be a family again. Besides, he had a nurse taking care of him daily. He was going to be fine.

"Wow," Tobias exclaimed and looked out over the wide waterways. A couple of boats had anchored at a small deserted island in the middle of it and people were sitting on the decks, drinking beers, while others were swimming in the water. I still couldn't get over how hot it was and cranked up the AC in the car. The thermometer in the car said ninety degrees. Ninety! In December?

I smiled and drove on, reminding myself to send Sara a postcard. She had been so jealous when she realized where we were going. I couldn't blame her. This looked more and more like true paradise to me.

Google Maps told me to follow the road across one more bridge, then continue through Cape Canaveral, and finally, we drove into Cocoa Beach. There was a statue of Kelly Slater at the entrance to Downtown Cocoa Beach. It had a bandage on its foot. I chuckled.

"What?" Julie asked. "What's so funny?"

"The statue," I said and pointed.

"Who's that?"

"He's the eleven-time world champion in surfing," I said. "And from Cocoa Beach. They're very proud of him. He recently hurt his foot, I read, and is out for the season, so they gave the statue a bandage on the foot. Cute."

Julie shrugged. "If you say so."

We drove through a row of small sixties-inspired

houses on each side. There was a restaurant that called itself Slow & Low, another called The Pig and the Whistle, and Mainly Lobster before we reached an intersection that looked like it was the center of town. A small café called Juice 'N Java was packed with people. They were eating sandwiches and drinking iced coffee. The jazz club next to it caught my interest. I had read it was in the top twenty jazz clubs in the U.S. I had secretly planned to go there with Sune one night but I still hadn't figured out how to find a babysitter for the little ones. Still, I was determined to find a way. We needed it. We needed to look each other in the eyes and remember why we fell in love. The patient-caregiver relationship made it hard for us to look at each other otherwise.

"Where is our house?" Tobias asked, jumping excitedly in the back seat. He never was good at sitting still and the ten hours in an airplane hadn't been good for him. He was about to explode with energy.

"Just five minutes down the road," I said.

We had looked at the area on Google back home, so we knew what it looked like, but it was still fun to see in real life.

"There it is!" Tobias exclaimed and pointed between Sune and me. "Over there!"

I drove up to the gate, punched in the code, and let it slowly open. The house was massive. Even bigger than I had imagined back home. Five bedrooms and a pool. Cost me eight thousand dollars for the month, but it was worth every penny.

"Whoa," Tobias said as the big pink house emerged in front of us. I was quite impressed myself.

I parked in the driveway as the gate closed behind me, then turned off the engine.

"Boys and girls, we're here."

7

"I want the biggest room!"

Julie and Tobias both stormed out the door. I had told them the code to the front door and let them go ahead, while I unstrapped William and let him follow them, running with his arms stretched out, shrieking loudly.

I walked to the back, grabbed Sune's wheelchair and got it out, then walked to him and helped him get into it. He had gotten a lot better at getting around using only his arms and most times he even refused my help. He didn't like being helpless and that made him fight to be self-sufficient. I had to say, I was very impressed with his courage and guts. I had often thought about how I would have reacted to this, had it been me, and I was pretty sure I would just have curled up in the fetal position and cried and never left the house again.

"I was here first!"

Julie was yelling from upstairs as I entered the big house and wheeled Sune across the tiles.

"I claimed this room first. Now, get out, Will!"

I sighed. William could be quite annoying when he wanted to and Julie had very little patience with him.

"William, you're sleeping downstairs with us," I yelled. "There are two rooms down here only separated by one door. You'll be with us."

I heard him on the stairs.

"Mooom," he said accusatorily, and even crying a little for my sympathy. "Juju and Tobby are *teas-ding* me."

William spoke with his pacifier still in his mouth and the words sounded funny. I had tried to get rid of the thing for months but he refused to give it up, even though we tried to hang it on a tree or said he could mail it to Santa. This month was going to be the one when I succeeded. I had made a deal with him that he could give it to Santa in person, then Santa would give him whatever he wanted for Christmas. I feared he would ask for an iPhone because both of his siblings had phones. I didn't want my four-year-old son to have a phone, but if that was the only way I could get him to give up his beloved binky, then I guess I'd have to cave in.

Now, all we had to do was to find Santa.

"Come down here. I have the perfect room for you," I said and let go of Sune's chair. He rolled it forward himself as he did most of the time. It was only when he got tired that I took over.

"Look at that view," he said.

"I know," I said and looked myself. It was really spectacular. Even more so than what I had seen in the pictures online. The house was old, from the seventies or so, had ten-foot ceilings and beautiful old Spanish tiles throughout the entire house. The kitchen was newer but still old-fashioned and cozy.

"This place is perfect for Christmas," I said.

Sune wheeled to the corner of the living room and the big fireplace.

"The tree can go right here," he said, smiling. His eyes were exhausted from the long trip, but he was happier than he had been for months, maybe even years. He had been talking about coming here for so long I could hardly remember a time he hadn't. It felt so good to finally be able to give him what he'd dreamt of.

"Then Santa can come down the chimney," Tobias said. He had just come down the stairs and was holding William's hand.

Sune's and my eyes met. I knew we were thinking the same thing: *he still believes in Santa?*

"Sure," I said, not knowing if the boy was just pretending to believe because of his younger brother or if he somehow had managed to keep the magic alive. Julie didn't believe anymore. At least, I didn't think she did. She never talked about it anymore.

I walked to the fireplace and looked up. Yup. It was real and not one of those fake ones. It even looked like it had been used recently.

"We better not light a fire, then," I said, smiling to Sune. "You know, just in case."

8

It had been a very long time since I last slept this well. The bed in the master bedroom at the rented house was awesome. Whether it was the mattress, the fresh ocean breeze, or just the fact that I was exhausted from the flight, I don't know. It didn't matter. I woke up just as the sun peeked over the horizon and its rays hit my face through the window. I felt rested and ready for a day in paradise.

Sune was still sleeping, so I grabbed my sneakers and went for a run on the beach. The sun was still rising and created a beautiful light outside and in the sparkling water. Pelicans were fishing, dropping from the sky into the ocean. I couldn't believe how hot it already was at six-thirty in the morning, but I had barely run for five minutes before I broke into a sweat. I was used to being freezing for the first twenty minutes and the cold air hurting my throat. This felt like heaven.

If I lived in a place like this, I would run every day, I

thought to myself, wiping sweat off my forehead with the back of my hand.

It was quite a surprise to me to notice that one of the houses I ran past actually had smoke coming from the chimney.

Who has a fire when it's eighty-two degrees in the morning?

Thinking they were crazy Americans, I shook my head, turned the music up on my Apple watch, and sang along while running toward downtown Cocoa Beach. There were a couple of surfers out in the water, sitting on their boards waiting for a wave, and others about to join them getting ready on the beach, waxing boards and putting on leashes. I noticed that none of them were wearing wet-suits. The water had to be warm too. I decided I would go for a swim after my run. Back home, when preparing for the trip, I had looked at my bikini a little disapprovingly. I refused to believe that it was actually going to be warm enough to go in the water since I liked my water warm, but Julie had told me to bring it. She had googled it and knew it was going to be warm. I was still skeptical, but now, as I was sweating along on my run, I was happy that for once I had listened to my dear daughter. I was looking forward to a dip in the Atlantic Ocean.

I ran past a couple of restaurants with decks that had views over the ocean, then continued all the way to the Cocoa Beach Pier before I made my turn. More surfers sat out there by the pier in the glistening sunlight and made me wish I had brought my camera.

Thinking about the camera made me worry about Sune once again. I wondered if he was ever going to get back to his passion, back into photography again. Not only was it his profession in life, it was also his great love. He never went anywhere without his camera and he always saw the most beautiful patterns in things that I couldn't see until he showed me. It was a gift. And he used to be the one who took all the pictures wherever we went, and especially of the kids, but since he'd been shot, he hadn't even wanted to touch his camera. In the beginning, I had told myself it was a phase, that he would soon get back to his old normal self again, but I had only been kidding myself. Deep down, I knew an event like this was bound to change you. I couldn't blame him for it, not even for his bad moods from time to time that he would sometimes take out on me in a bad way. But after two years of things being this way, I was getting worn out. Fact was, I needed this doctor to fix him just as much as he did. I needed our lives back. I knew they would never be the same, but I needed things to move forward, to get better, to improve.

I needed hope.

9

Even though I was playing loud music, I still heard the screams. They were so ear piercing that I immediately stopped running, pulled off my headset, and looked in the direction they came from.

It was the house with the smoke in the chimney.

"What the...?"

I walked up the beach toward the house. A woman opened the sliding door leading to the wooden porch and staggered outside, gasping for air, dropped to her knees, then threw up.

As soon as she was done, I heard her moan and scream, then cry and moan again, sounding like an animal in distress. I ran to her.

"Do you need help?" I said.

The woman didn't answer. She didn't even look up at me. Snot was gushing out of her nose and mouth as she cried and gasped almost inhumanly. I wondered if she was having a seizure of sorts and knelt next to her.

"Can I help you? Ma'am? Do you need any medicine or anything?"

There were more screams coming from inside the house. I wondered if I had walked into some sort of domestic dispute, if the woman was in trouble somehow.

"Who's in there?" I asked. "Is that your husband? Do you need me to call for help?"

The woman finally looked up at me, her eyes terrified, as she grabbed me with both her hands, clinging to me like I was her last hope.

"My son," she said.

"Your son? Is he in there? Is he in trouble?"

The woman gasped for air and searched for words, but none came, only strange gurgling sounds coming from deep within her throat. I didn't want to wait for her to explain any further. I used my watch to dial 911.

"What's your emergency?" the dispatcher said.

I gave my name and told them I was from Denmark on vacation and how I had found the woman and that I knew she needed help but I didn't know what was going on exactly since the woman could hardly explain it to me. The dispatcher told me to try and get something out of her, so I addressed the woman once again.

"You mentioned your son," I said. "Is he in trouble?"

The woman's nostrils were flaring. "I...how was I supposed to know? That he would..."

"How were you supposed to know what?" I asked. "You've got to tell me a little more here."

"That he would...that he would crawl up...there?"

The woman looked toward the chimney. The black

smoke was still emerging from it and it had gotten darker and now it started to smell. It took me a few seconds to put the pieces together, mostly because it seemed so very unlikely a scenario.

The terror of it almost paralyzed me. "Your...your son...he's...up in there?" I asked and pointed.

The woman sank, then nodded. "He was looking for Santa," she said. "I think he got stuck."

10

The firefighters came very fast and fought to get the boy out. It was the scene of a nightmare, a pure horror movie as they pulled from the bottom, then lowered someone down the chimney to push him out, and finally managed to pull him out, his charcoaled body unrecognizable. Only his face and shoulders had remained untouched by the fire.

I held her in my arms till it was over while her husband held their teenage daughter close and covered her eyes so she didn't have to watch. I didn't know much about what was happening but I couldn't help but wonder if the poor woman had lit the fire in the fireplace herself this morning, thinking it would make the morning cozier for them all at Christmas time. Had the boy been asleep or maybe unconscious from lack of air? Had he been stuck there all night, hoping and praying someone would find him, maybe even calling for them, calling for his mother?

No matter how I thought of it, it was terrifying and utterly, absolutely devastating.

No mother should have to go through a thing like this.

I gave the police my testimony and the paramedics cared for the mother. The detective in charge took my phone number and told me he would be in touch. I stared, baffled, as the family—or what was left of it—were taken away in an ambulance to the emergency room for observation. The look in their eyes shook me violently and I ran as fast as I could back to the house, threw off my shoes, and stormed into the kitchen where the kids were sitting.

I had called them from my watch and told them to help Sune get out of bed, that I would explain later, and to make themselves some breakfast. We had shopped on the way there the day before so there should be enough food for all of them. Plenty of milk and cereal and also bread if they needed toast.

The kids stared at me as I entered.

"Where were you?" Julie asked angrily. "We had to do everything around here."

She was feeding William next to her. The boy lit up when he saw my face.

"Mommy!"

I walked to him, took him in my arms and held him tight, then walked to Julie and Tobias and pulled them all into a hug. "You have no idea how glad I am to see all of you," I said.

Julie pulled out of my embrace with a grunt. "Mom. That's annoying. Where were you?"

"There was an accident. In one of the beach houses further down. A kid was killed."

I avoided the gory details since I didn't see any reason to provide them.

"What happened?" Sune asked.

"It was an accident," I said. "But I had to help the mother and wait till the police and paramedics came and got the boy out."

Julie turned and looked at me. "Got the boy out?"

"Yeah, well...he was stuck somewhere; let's just leave it at that."

"Where was he stuck, Mom?" Julie asked.

She had lately developed a flavor for the horrific and liked to watch horror shows on her computer and read scary books. I wasn't so fond of her newfound joy for frightening things but considered it more or less a part of her growing independence since she knew I didn't enjoy it.

"You don't need to know that," I said.

Her gaze was overwhelmed with fascination. "No. Tell me, Mom. Where was the boy stuck?"

I made a grimace for her to stop. I didn't want William to hear any of it, and frankly, not her either. She was too young.

"Tell me, Mom, where was he? I bet it was a nasty place. Did he die from suffocation?"

I stared at my daughter. Where had all this come from? Her father? It had to be because it sure wasn't me. I had seen my share of horrific stories and deaths; I didn't exactly enjoy talking about them.

"Where, Mom. Where?"

She saw me look at William, then she covered his ears with her hands. "He won't hear it. Heck, he won't even understand anything. Just tell me, Mom. Come on."

I sighed, then said: "No. Now, if you'll excuse me, I'll take a shower. I smell awful and feel even worse after what I have seen."

I passed the fireplace, then shivered.

Julie's eyes lit up like fireworks. "It was the chimney, wasn't it?" she clapped her hands in excitement. "It was the chimney. The boy was stuck in the...and then they...oh."

I bit my lip.

"I'll be in the shower if anyone needs me," I said.

11

The shower didn't help. The smell and the images of the charcoaled body wouldn't leave, no matter how much I scrubbed and washed. The smell was in my hair and in my nostrils. At least that's how I felt.

Sune rolled into the bedroom and shut the door behind him, then approached me.

"What the heck was that?"

I sighed and sat on the bed. "I don't know." I looked at my hands. They were still shaking. "I am completely in shock still."

"No, I'm talking about with Julie? Why did you tell her? I didn't want Tobias to know something like that and he was there too, so was William."

I looked at him, our gaze meeting across the room. He had that look in his eyes I had grown to know so well. He was angry. It happened from time to time that he felt bitter and lost hope and then he would take it out on me.

"I hardly think William understood anything. Besides, Julie guessed it."

"And you don't think Tobias did too? He's not as stupid as you think, my friend."

My friend. He always called me that when he had one of his *episodes* as I called them. It happened about once a week or so; he would yell at me for the smallest things. I had let him do it because I felt so sorry for him, but it hurt just the same.

"I can't do this right now, Sune," I said with a deep sigh, then walked to my suitcase to grab my clothes.

Sune scoffed. "You can never do anything, can you? Do I have to remind you that I'm the one sitting in a wheelchair, huh? I'm the one who can't move, and for every day, for every hour that passes that I haven't gotten back up again, the probability of me doing so shrinks."

"We've been through this, Sune," I said and dropped my shirt. I turned to look at him. "We've done everything we can, okay? We've been through all kinds of physical therapy, all kinds of doctors. What else would you have me do?"

Sune looked perplexed. He was yelling now. "I don't know. Something! I'm dying here. I'm withering away in this thing. If I don't get out of it soon, I will never leave this chair again. It's been two years, Rebekka. TWO years."

"I know it has. You keep reminding me. And I am doing everything I can to help you." I picked up the shirt once again and looked for a hanger in the closet.

"Do you have any idea how humiliating it is to have

your son and stepdaughter help you out of bed in the morning? Huh? My son is eleven years old. I should be the one to help him out of bed, not the other way around. Do you understand how terrible that made me feel?"

I turned to look at him again. I was so tired of fighting with him. I had hoped it wouldn't happen while we were on this trip, the trip he had been asking for, for so long. I had hoped that the prospect of seeing this doctor would spark the hope in him and he would feel less bitter and have fewer episodes. But I also knew that he was nervous about meeting him tomorrow. I knew he was and that made him angry.

"I am sorry, Sune. I really am. But I had to help the woman and her family. It was an accident, Sune. I would have been back in time to help you if this hadn't happened."

"Excuses. There's always something, isn't there? How do I even know that what you're telling me is true? You come home here with this story of a child stuck..."

"HEY!"

It was my turn to yell now. I no longer cared that the kids could hear us. "I have just been a witness to a terrible accident. I feel awful. I can't deal with this right now," I said as I threw my shirt back in the suitcase and left the room, slamming the door behind me.

12

Sydney Hahn was eating dinner with her mom and younger sister Trisha. On the calendar in the kitchen, it said December 2nd. On the calendar, there was a big picture of Santa. It felt like he was laughing at her, mocking her.

She had dreaded this month all year.

"Do you girls know what you want for Christmas this year?" Their mom asked. She was trying to sound cheerful, but not succeeding very well.

Trisha looked up, eyes big. "I'm wishing for a new bike."

"Good," their mom said without looking at her. She had hardly eaten anything, only pushed the peas around the potatoes on her plate. She had done that a lot and lost a lot of weight the past year.

"How about you, Sydney?" she asked, drinking from her glass of water. "Do you have any wishes or are you too old for that now that you're a teenager?"

"Very funny," she said.

"What's it like?" Trisha asked. "To be a teenager?"

Sydney shrugged. "I don't know."

"You must know since you are one," her sister reminded her.

"Yeah, well, it's not like you wake up one day and you're suddenly different just because you turned thirteen," she said. "It kind of just sneaks up on you, I guess. I don't feel any different."

"I see it," her sister said. "You're texting more and you keep more to yourself in your room and you're on the computer more and sometimes I hear you cry. Is it because you're a teenager that you cry?"

Sydney dropped her fork onto the plate. "Mo-om!"

"That's enough, girls," their mother said. It was obvious she hadn't listened to anything they had said. She got up and put her plate in the sink with a sigh. On the wall hung a picture of all four of them.

"Where are we going to celebrate Christmas?" Trisha asked, chewing with her mouth open.

"Don't do that," Sydney said.

"Don't do what?" Trisha said.

"Chew with your mouth open."

"I can chew with my mouth open if I want to, right Mommy?" she said and opened her mouth even wider so Sydney could see everything.

Sydney grabbed her plate and got up. "That's it, I've lost my appetite."

"So, where are we going for Christmas?" Trisha asked again.

Sydney stopped to listen. Last year, they hadn't even celebrated it at all. Their mother had been in her bed all through Christmas, crying. Would they even celebrate this year?

"What's that?" their mother asked when she realized their eyes were on her.

"Christmas, Mom," Sydney said. "Do we celebrate it this year?"

Her eyes grew absent. "Sure, yes, no, of course we do. Maybe you two should make your lists for Santa, huh?"

Sydney stopped at the mention of his name. She bit her lip and looked in the direction of the fireplace. She believed she could hear it again. It had started the day before, on December 1st. Like a low rumble, a beat or a pulse of sorts coming from inside the chimney. And then there were the bells. The sound of sleigh bells.

Sydney closed her eyes and shook her head. When she opened her eyes, the sound was gone.

"I just wish Dad could come back," she said, then left.

13

I MADE A NICE DINNER. I drove to Publix and shopped while feeling awful. I bought some lamb chops and cooked them on the grill with lots of garlic and served it with rice and an Indian curry sauce. It was Sune's favorite dish. I guess I was feeling bad about our fight and what was supposed to be the beginning of a wonderful vacation for us. I tried to make him happy and I succeeded. After a few hours alone in the bedroom, he had come out and was finally smiling and grabbed my hand across the table.

"I'm sorry," he mouthed.

"Me too," I said, feeling relieved.

I hated fighting and ever since Sune had been shot, I had felt so guilty, so responsible for his happiness, it was beginning to make me miserable. I knew he was only nervous about meeting the doctor tomorrow and that was why he freaked out earlier. After tomorrow, it would all be better. I was certain it would. This doctor was going to change everything. He simply had to.

"How was the ocean?" I asked the kids. They had been on the beach all afternoon, swimming in the ocean and building sandcastles.

"Awesome," Tobias said.

"Too sandy," Julie said, making a grimace.

William just gave me a grin showing a piece of half-eaten meat.

I looked at my daughter. "You usually love the beach?"

She shook her head. "Too much sun."

"We don't like the sun now?"

"Too bright," she said.

Where was this coming from? My daughter always loved the beach and the ocean. I hadn't expected these teenage-like attitudes from her for at least two more years. Was it starting so soon? At only eleven? Or was she just acting out because it had been a rough couple of years because so much of my attention went to Sune or William? I couldn't blame her, really. She had also lost her dad at a very young age; I had to count that in as well.

"Well, maybe it'll be better tomorrow," I said and sipped my red wine.

"I'm not going to the beach tomorrow," she said, grabbed her plate, and got up.

"What? Why not? I thought we could all go after we go to the doctor's office."

"Well, I'm not going down there again."

"Why not?"

She shrugged and put her plate in the sink.

"She wants to play Roblox," Tobias said. "With Thomas F."

"Oh. And who is Thomas F?" I asked.

Julie gave Tobias a look. "I hate you," she said.

"Hey, hey. That's not how you speak to your brother," I said.

Julie stomped her feet on the tiles. "He's NOT my brother. You guys aren't even married."

That stung. And she knew it. It was the issue no one spoke of, except for Julie. The issue of marriage. I wasn't sure I wanted to get married again. Not after how badly it had ended last time. But Sune was different, I sensed. He wanted it. He wanted the wedding and the party and the paperwork stating that we belonged together.

Julie grunted angrily and walked away.

"You're not spending the entire day on your computer playing with some boy!" I yelled after her, but she had already gone up the stairs and slammed the door.

I turned to face Tobias. "Okay, tell me everything. Who is Thomas F?"

14

She had a nightmare and woke with a start. Sydney felt her heart racing in her chest and wondered if it was possible for it to actually jump out. She had dreamt about her father again. She missed him so much that it literally hurt from time to time.

Sydney turned on the light and went to her computer then turned it on. It had become a habit of hers to sit on the computer all night when the rest of her family was asleep. It was mostly because of the nightmares. She couldn't fall asleep afterward.

They were always the same. She was in the car with her dad on the day he died, driving down the road, talking, chatting, and laughing like they always did when they were alone.

And then they crashed. But it wasn't the crash that was scary, it was the sensation she felt right before he hit the tree. The feeling of dread and fear, and then the laughter. Someone was laughing.

Sydney shook her head to get rid of the feeling the dream had left her with. She hadn't been in the car when her dad crashed into the tree, but ever since she had started dreaming about it, she hadn't been able to escape the thought that something else had happened to him. It was no ordinary crash.

Lately, she had spent hours searching the web, trying to figure out more. Sydney had gotten quite skilled at entering places on the computer that most people could never access and she had read the police report of her dad's crash about a hundred times, going over every little detail.

It was precisely one year ago this month that he left the prison outside of Orlando, where he had been evaluating some woman's mental state in order to determine if she was fit for a trial or not. Sydney knew all the details since she had gone over it again and again. Her mother didn't understand why she couldn't just let it go, but she couldn't. There was something odd about her father's death and she couldn't let it go. Her dad was an excellent driver. There were no other cars on the road. Why would he suddenly crash into a tree on the side of the road?

Suicide, the police had speculated and asked them questions about him, whether he was depressed or ever talked about killing himself. It was ridiculous to Sydney. Her dad was never depressed. Maybe he wasn't the happiest man on the planet, but he would never kill himself. He would never leave his girls like that.

Sydney opened the documents once again, hacking into the Cocoa Beach Police Department's main server and finding them. She looked at the report written by the detective Jack Ryder, who she had talked to back when he had come to their house and told them what had happened.

He had annoyed her so much with his long blond hair and handsome smile and the way he talked about her father as if he was a completely different person than what he was.

"You don't know him!" she had ended up yelling at him.

"It's okay," he said addressed to her mother, who had yelled at her for yelling at the detective. "It's only natural to respond with anger in a situation like this. It can be tough for a young girl to grasp. It's tough."

It's tough, pah, what did he know about anything? Mr. Pretty and Handsome probably had a beautiful wife and a perfect life.

But he had provided an excuse for Sydney's mother, one that could explain just about anything Sydney did. She would use it whenever she got angry at something.

"It's the grief talking."

She even used that excuse when Sydney had come to her showing her the picture of her dad's dead body from the police file, pointing at his neck and at the red marks on it.

"It's just the grief. You want an explanation, someone to blame. We all do, but the fact is, your dad killed himself."

But Sydney knew better. She knew he hadn't killed

himself and she had devoted all of her time awake at night to figuring out what happened to him.

Sydney zoomed in on the picture once again so she could see the two red marks on his neck. She had seen enough vampire movies to know exactly what those marks were.

15

"I can't believe she has a boyfriend," I said to Sune while getting ready for bed.

"What's that?" Sune was reading his book. I had bathed him and helped him into his jammies, then helped him get into bed. I always took care of him first.

"Thomas F," I said.

"Who's that?"

"What do you mean, who's that? Thomas F. Tobias just told us everything about him at dinner."

"Ah, that," Sune said.

"Can you believe her? I mean, she's only eleven. Isn't she kind of young to have a boyfriend?"

Sune shrugged. I crawled under the covers and sat next to him. When we sat like that in bed, it was almost as if everything was back to normal, back to before Sune was shot.

"You don't think it's early?" I asked, surprised.

"I had my first girlfriend when I was ten."

"Of course, you did," I said and grabbed my book. I read a couple of pages that I didn't even care about, then breathed heavily. Sune looked up from his book.

"You just won't let it go, will you?"

"Why hasn't she told me about him? We always tell each other everything. Is she suddenly keeping stuff from me?"

"Not stuff. Just one boy," Sune said. "Don't make a big deal out of this, please, I'm begging you. It's not like it's a real boyfriend. They haven't even met in real life."

"No, but they meet online every day," Tobias told me. "I don't like it."

"Tobias told us the guy lives far away, like at the other end of the country. I don't think there's any danger in having an online boyfriend. It's not like anything is going to happen."

"How do you know?" I asked. "How do we even know he's a kid? He could be some pervert."

"If they talk on Skype every day and play Roblox together, don't you think Julie would have found out?"

I looked down at my book, then back up. "I don't know. I mean, I've heard about these guys who are really good at luring kids. They pretend to be teenagers and then..."

"She should be able to hear it in his voice and see his face when they Skype each other."

I nodded. "True."

I returned to my book and Sune to his. I read two more pages, then sighed. Sune rolled his eyes.

"Now what?"

"It's just..."

"What?"

"I just don't like it," I said. "I have no way of controlling what this guy says to our daughter. What if he asks to meet her?"

"Julie is not that stupid," he said. "Please, can't you just let this go?" He put his book on the side table, then turned off his lamp. "I want to go to sleep now. I have an important day tomorrow."

I looked at Sune as he closed his eyes. Back in the day, he would never go to sleep without kissing me first. Now, I didn't even want him to. What had happened to us?

"Yes," I said and turned off my own lamp. "Starting tomorrow, everything will get better."

16

SYDNEY WAS IMMERSED in reading the police report when she heard it. At first, it was more like a sensation than an actual sound. Like a deep rumble inside of her chest. She held a hand to her throat and breathed in deep gasps. Her doctor had told her she might experience physical symptoms of her loss and that's what she thought it was.

Sydney tried to ignore it, to begin with, but the sensation grew stronger, and soon she had to get up from her desk. She tried hard to calm herself down since it felt like everything was on fire inside of her.

"I need something to drink," she said and left the room.

She walked carefully so she wouldn't make a noise across the creaking floors in the hallway and on the stairs. The last thing she wanted was to wake up her sister and especially their mother. She wasn't sleeping well either, not since the accident. Often, Sydney could hear her crying in her bed, probably thinking it was a good time to cry since both kids were asleep.

Sydney sneaked into the kitchen, grabbed a glass, and filled it with water from the fridge. Feeling hungry, she grabbed a banana and ate it too, while looking outside at the street lamp where bugs were dancing in the light. She swallowed the last bite, then heard a noise.

The sound of sleigh bells.

She walked into the living room, then stared at the fireplace and the chimney. The sound grew louder as she approached it. Somehow, it was attracting her to it, calling for her to come closer.

"W-who's there?" she asked.

It almost sounded like a rhythm. Sydney stared at the chimney where the sound seemed to come from.

But that's impossible.

Sydney swallowed, hard. It was pitch dark inside the living room. She stood in the doorway and listened to the sound, not knowing what to do. She wanted to get closer, to look up inside the chimney to see what it was. Maybe it was an animal? Maybe it got stuck somehow?

But she knew it was no animal. Because she had heard the same sound before. And no animals made the sound of sleigh bells jingling.

Sydney felt a prickle of sweat on her upper lip and wiped it with her hand. She could hear her own ragged breaths. Something about that sound was so terrifying she could hardly stand it.

"W-who is it? Is someone there?"

Now, the sound was louder. And it felt like it was answering her, communicating with her.

Sydney shook her head, then backed away from the chimney.

No. I am not doing this. I am not seriously talking to my chimney. This can't be happening.

She turned on her heel and stormed up the stairs, crept under the covers and stayed under them, repeating to herself while still hearing the bells jingle from downstairs:

"I am not going insane I am not going insane. I am NOT!"

17

Doctor Herman's office was located on Merritt Island about twenty minutes' drive from the house where we were staying. It was on the island between our barrier island and the mainland and quite a spectacular drive there, over the bridge and the wide waters.

I, for one, was in a terrific mood, looking forward to finally giving Sune what he had been dreaming of for so long. And maybe, just maybe, making him happy and hopeful about the future.

Sune was in the seat next to me, biting his nails, while the kids were all in the back. I hoped the doctor's office would have someplace they could sit while we spoke to the doctor since it would be hard for us to concentrate properly with them around us. I had loaded up on iPads, Nintendo Gameboys, and even brought Julie's computer, so they could all keep themselves entertained. I didn't know how long it was going to take, but I had a feeling it might take a while since I assumed they would need to have Sune assessed in the gym first before making a judgment whether they would be able to help him. I had no idea what came after if they said yes, but thought I would have to figure that one out once we got to it. One issue at a time. The first hurdle was to get the doctor to even see us, then we'd have to take it from there.

That's what I told myself, but inside I was, of course, worried like crazy about the outcome and trying to imagine different scenarios. I mean, I really wanted for Sune to see this doctor and I really wanted him to want to take him on as a patient and promise him he could help him since he was known to have had great success with cases like Sune's, but what if he did? What if he actually said he would take him? We were only here for a month. I was guessing he couldn't fix Sune that fast. I knew it would take months, if not years of intensive training. How were we supposed to afford it? The treatment and the travel? We would have to travel to the U.S. on a monthly basis probably. There was no way we could afford that.

"It's here," Sune said and pointed at the sign. "I recognize the picture from his website."

I looked out the window and saw the billboard on the side of the road outside a huge building with riverfront views. On the billboard, Dr. Herman smiled at the people passing by. It was quite remarkable and a little over the top for my taste.

I didn't say anything, but drove into the parking lot and parked the car. The kids rushed out of the car while I helped Sune get into his chair.

"Don't do that," Sune hissed at me when I grabbed his arm. "You know I don't like it when you do it like that."

"Sorry," I said and pulled back.

I hated when I did something wrong, and I almost always did, especially when he was anxious.

He's just nervous, Rebekka. He's just nervous. We all are.

William bumped into my leg and hugged it tightly, reacting to a sudden childish desire to hug his mommy that needed to be fulfilled right away, but as he did, he pushed me into Sune, who almost slipped when trying to swing his body into the chair next to the car.

"Damn it!" Sune yelled.

"I'm sorry," I said again, then grabbed William in my arms and took a step away.

"Control that stupid kid, will you?"

William started to cry.

Oh, boy.

Julie rolled her eyes and turned away from us, while Tobias looked like he could cry himself while gazing at his helpless dad. I handed him William, who was still crying, then attended to Sune. I lifted him into his chair even though it killed my back, put him down, then walked to William and grabbed him in my arms, comforting him, telling him his dad didn't really mean it, that he wasn't stupid. When he finally stopped crying, I looked at Julie and Tobias.

"All right, kids. I need you to be on your best behavior for the next couple of hours, all right? This is important. To all of us. Can I count on you?"

Tobias nodded and, after a little while, Julie nodded reluctantly as well.

Holding William on my hip, pushing Sune in his chair, ignoring all my body's signs of pain and stress, I marched ahead toward the entrance to what—hopefully—would change our lives for the better.

18

Of course, it took forever before it was our turn. We waited an hour past our appointment time. And then there was the paperwork. We had to fill out so many forms, my hand hurt in the end.

Finally, we were told to come into the examination room, where we met a young man who apparently wasn't Dr. Herman, but someone else who talked to Sune really quickly, then examined his legs and his back, putting him up on a stretcher. He didn't talk to me at all or tell us anything, just grumbled some sounds when asking Sune to do several things, which he, of course, couldn't do. Then the young man left and we were asked to go back into the waiting room.

I could tell Sune felt disappointed. He didn't speak a word to any of us while we waited, and his eyes avoided mine. I knew how devastated he must have felt since he couldn't do any of the exercises the man had asked him to.

Half an hour later, we were told to come back in again, into an office with a big redwood desk.

"Dr. Herman will be right with you," the nurse said.

I hoped she was right. We had left the three kids in the waiting room. Julie and Tobias were in charge of William and I could only pray that it would go well. There were some children's books in there that he could flip through, but other than that, it wasn't a very child-friendly place.

They're fine. The big kids will take care of him.

The door opened and the man from the billboard entered, but he wasn't smiling like he was out there. He looked seriously at Sune when he greeted us and shook our hands. Then, he sighed.

It wasn't a good sound.

He looked down into Sune's file, then back up at him. "I don't know what to tell you," he said.

You don't know? You're the one who is supposed to know! You're the one who's the doctor here; you're the one we traveled almost five thousand miles to see. And now you tell us you don't know?

I wanted to yell it out, but of course, I didn't. Instead, I simply said:

"What do you mean, Doctor?"

"What I mean is, I'm looking at the file here with all the information you sent us, the x-rays and doctor's evaluation, and I see no reason for you to not be walking by now."

I almost choked. "Excuse me?"

"Listen. I know it might be a lot to take in, but you *can* walk, Sune."

Sune huffed. "I...I really can't."

Doctor Herman leaned over his desk, then closed Sune's file. "It's all in your head, young man. It happens sometimes; people mentally block themselves like this. But you can walk, I'm telling you. I have seen a ton of cases like yours. You can walk. But you've got to get out of that head of yours."

"Excuse me?" I said, feeling rage envelop me. Who was this guy? Who did he think he was? "My boyfriend was shot in the spine two years ago. Every doctor we have ever spoken to has told us Sune will never walk again. We've tried everything, every training program and treatment we could find. They all said the same thing. He will never walk again."

Dr. Herman turned and looked at me, then shrugged, tapping the corner of Sune's file on the desk.

"Well, they were wrong."

"What?" I said. "How can you...who are you to..."

Sune reached out his hand to stop me. "Rebekka. It's okay." He looked at the doctor. "Can you help me, Doctor?"

He shook his head. "I'm afraid not."

I could feel Sune's disappointment in the room.

"It's not that I don't want to," the doctor said. "But you need to make the first move. You have to start moving your toes first. Even a wiggle would do. You are the one with the mental block. You need to get past that first.

Then I can help you." He smiled politely at both of us, then looked at his watch. "I have another patient. Come back and see me when you've made progress, okay?"

19

IF PEOPLE COULD ACTUALLY EXPLODE, I would have done it by now. I was furious as we drove back home. Sune sitting next to me didn't utter a word, whereas I couldn't stop talking.

"Who does he think he is? Telling you that you can already walk, it's all in your head. Is that really what we traveled five thousand miles for? Not to mention the cost of seeing this guy. What a quack. I can't believe it."

"What happened?" Tobias asked.

Julie had given up and was sitting with her headphones on, listening to music from her phone. William had fallen asleep. He had managed to rip several magazines to pieces and drizzled the pieces all over the waiting room area without Tobias and Julie even noticing it until it was too late. The lady behind the counter had shot me a look when we finally came back out, but I had given her one back that had made hers fade in comparison.

I looked in the rearview mirror at Tobias.

"Didn't he want to treat my dad?" he continued.

I didn't know how to answer that. I mean, how much did the boy need to know? He was, after all, just that, only a boy. A young boy with hopes and dreams of one day getting his father back.

"He said not now. Maybe later," I answered, then looked briefly at Sune, who hadn't uttered a word since the visit at the doctor's office. He was looking out the window at the scenery as we drove across the bridge and back to the barrier island.

"So, what do we do now?" Tobias asked, his voice cracking. I could hardly bear it. Sune still didn't react, so I guessed it was up to me to calm the poor boy down.

"Now, I say we get some lunch," I said and looked at the clock in the car. It was almost three o'clock. No wonder I was starving. The kids had to be too. I spotted the golden M in the distance.

"How about some Mac D?"

"Ew." Julie took out her headphones. "McDonald's is like the grossest thing in the world. You know they fill those burgers with so many preservatives that they never get old, right? I saw this Vine about a guy who had saved his burger for two years and it didn't grow any mold at all."

I sighed. I wasn't a big fan of fast food myself, but in this particular situation, we just needed an easy solution.

"Okay then," I said. "What do you suggest?"

"There was a nice little café on the corner downtown when we're almost at the house. It was called something with juice or something."

"I hardly think Sune is in the mood to sit and eat at a café," I said. "Can't you find something else?"

"Why does everything have to be about him all the time?" Julie asked.

"JULIE!"

She paused with a sigh. She knew she had overstepped a line. "I'm just sayin'," she added.

"Julie. I don't want to hear another word from you right now, or there will be no more computer for the rest of this trip, do you read me?"

Finally, Sune reacted. He held his hand up in the air. "I think it sounds like a great idea. I could do with a good sandwich right about now."

I looked at him, startled. I thought he'd be too devastated to do anything...maybe even for the rest of the trip. This was a good sign, and I immediately turned into the café's parking lot.

Juice 'N Java, the sign said, and just like the day we had arrived, it seemed to be packed with people.

20

We ordered and sat down outside, even though it was very hot. I had a sandwich with goat cheese and portabella mushroom, and it was quite good, to my surprise. I hadn't expected much food-wise when traveling to the States, but I guess we got lucky.

The kids had sandwiches and smoothies and Sune and I each had pumpkin lattes.

The place was crowded with people, even though it was situated directly out to A1A, the main road going through town along the beach.

In the middle of eating my sandwich, William knocked over his cup and spilled soda all over the table.

"William!" Julie shrieked and moved away, but not fast enough for her shirt to not get wet. She wailed in anger. "Now I'm soaked!"

"I'll get some napkins," I said and got up, thinking that would be the end of the peace. It was nice while it lasted. I almost made it through my entire sandwich.

Inside, I ran into the detective that I had met the day before. He smiled handsomely and I blushed.

Why am I blushing?

"Hello there," he said. He had a sandwich in his hands, wrapped to go.

"Late lunch?" I said.

He nodded. "Been a long day. How about you?"

I sighed. "You don't want to know. How's the case?"

"What case is that?"

"About the boy? From the chimney?" I felt terrible talking about it like it was an everyday thing. "Any news?"

He shrugged. "There really isn't much to it, other than what you saw."

I nodded, a little embarrassed. I was only trying to make conversation. "Of course not. It was an accident. The boy was excited to see Santa and probably crawled up there because he thought he might be there."

"That's what I figure. Don't see any reason to think otherwise."

"Terrible story, though."

He sipped his coffee. "Sure is," he said. "Now, if you'll excuse me, I have work to do." He nodded toward the door. I spotted the police station's sign on the building across the street.

"You work right over there, huh? That's convenient. Bet you come here every day, then."

He smiled. Our eyes met. Boy, he was handsome. "Pretty much," he said and walked away. "Pretty much."

As he opened the door, I was pulled back to reality, when I heard Julie yell—no, make that scream—at

William. I hurried to grab a stack of napkins then rushed back outside and handed them to her.

"My shirt is ruined, Mom. Completely ruined. I am never wearing this again. Never."

"Okay," I said, still watching the detective as he crossed the street. When he disappeared into the old building that also housed city hall, I turned and looked at them with a soft sigh.

"How about we go home now, huh? We can still get a couple of hours in at the pool."

Tobias and William both squealed with excitement.

PART II

21

Eight-year-old Kristin Walker loved singing more than anything else in this world. Even more than cookies and ice cream, even though they did come in at second place. There was only one other thing Kristin loved about Christmas almost as much as singing carols, and that was eating all the delicious Christmas candy and cookies.

Her mother, Patricia, had long tried to get her to lose weight, but Kristin just loved food so darn much; she couldn't stop once she started. And so it was this evening on December 3rd that she found herself in the kitchen, grabbing one of the freshly baked cookies her mother had just pulled out of the oven.

First, she grabbed one with her right hand, then another with her left.

One for each hand, like her grandfather had always said. He didn't say it anymore, though, because now he had gone up to be with God, her mother said. But Kristin had missed him so terribly when he went and had asked her mother why God wanted grandpop so badly when he had so many others he could hang out with, whereas Kristin only had one grandpop.

Her mother said she didn't have an answer for that.

"Kristin!"

Her mother had entered the kitchen and looked at the cookie sheet. "Did you eat any of the cookies?"

Still chewing, Kristin shook her head, hiding the other cookie behind her back. Her mother didn't believe her and wiped a crumb away from her lip with a loud *tsk* while shaking her head.

"How am I supposed to get you to fit into that dress for aunt Tina's wedding this spring, huh? She really wants you to be a flower girl, but only if you can fit into the dress," she said.

Kristin licked her lips and got ahold of another crumb. Then, she shrugged. Her mother held out her hand.

"Hand it over, Kristin."

Kristin sighed, then handed her the cookie that was mostly crumbs by now. Her mother took it all and threw the delicious cookie out, then wiped her daughter's face with a napkin and corrected the bow on her dress.

"Now, there, you look pretty. Now, remember, don't eat the cookies, all right? They're for tonight, to hand out to people while we sing for them."

Going around town caroling was a tradition that was repeated every year. One her mother had started. Kristin used to love it so much since everyone always told her how stunning her voice was, but last year hadn't been so much fun. Since she had gained so much weight, people stared at her, their faces making grimaces, some unable to even recognize her. They no longer focused on the singing, but on her size, and that bothered her. She wasn't looking forward to them doing it again this year.

"All right, now remember, we start out with *Silent Night* and we finish up with your solo of *Ave Maria*. Oh, it's a really good program this year. I can't wait to get out there and spread some holiday joy into people's homes. They sure need it these days, with all the stress and rushing going on. People are so busy; they need us to remind them to slow down and enjoy Christmas. It's a gift, Kristin, to be able to do that. One you should not look upon lightly, you hear me?"

Kristin nodded, her eyes only on the remaining cookies. She thought about two days ago when she had gone to the mall to sit on Santa's lap and he had grunted, strained by her weight.

Kristin loved Santa; even though some of her friends told her he wasn't real, she still believed he was. She knew perfectly well that the guy at the mall wasn't him, of course she did, but the real Santa was there, bringing presents to children. She knew he was. And she so hoped she would get to see him this year.

22

Sune hid in the bedroom for the rest of the afternoon. Meanwhile, I hung out with the kids in the pool, wondering what he was doing in there all alone while the kids and I, for once, were having a great time. Even Julie finally got over herself and got in and now she was splashing around with her siblings like they had never been fonder of one another.

I realized I was never going to understand those kids and figure them out. And maybe I didn't have to. Maybe it was enough to simply enjoy the good moments we did have and not worry about when the next fight or outburst would end up ruining everything.

Still, I couldn't stop thinking about Sune, and finally, after swimming with the kids for about an hour, I grabbed my towel and walked into the bedroom. Sune was sitting by the window, staring out at the ocean.

"Hey," I said. "What are you doing?"

"I told you to leave me alone," he said.

I dried my hair, wondering what to do, then approached him. "Sune. You can't shut me out like that. I know today was devastating but...are we never going to talk about what the doctor said?"

He lifted his head and looked into my eyes. "Didn't you think I could see you?"

I froze. "What do you mean?"

"With that guy. The policeman. Don't you think I saw you?"

"I...I...I don't know. It was just the detective from the accident yesterday morning. I was just asking if there was any news."

"You blushed. Your eyes avoided his in that cute way that I always found endearing. I saw it, Rebekka. I saw all of it."

"I...I..."

"It's all right," he said. "I know I've been acting awful lately. I know it can't be much fun to be with someone like me. I understand that you have needs too. Needs that I can't fulfill."

Oh, dear Lord.

"Sune. I love you. I don't care that you're in a wheelchair. I still love you the same."

"Really?"

"Really."

"Because it sure doesn't feel that way. Not when you were flirting with Blondie there."

"I wasn't flirting. I was asking about the case."

"What case? I thought it was an accident?"

"It is. It was. I mean...yes, but I just wanted to...I was

trying to be polite. I wasn't flirting. Besides, I'm sure he has a wife and kids and everything."

Sune scoffed. "Of course. You've already thought of that."

"No. I was just assuming...you know what? I am sick of having to justify myself. Yes, I found the guy attractive. I am sorry. I still love you, though. I'm still here with you, even though you treat me like dirt half of the time."

Sune paused. He looked at me, then shook his head. "I don't even know how we got here," he said. "How it got to this."

"Me either," I said. "I guess it just happened. I guess we let it happen."

Just as I said the words, the phone in my pocket rang. Startled, I picked it up. Sune scoffed. "It's probably him already, calling to take you out."

"Don't be ridiculous," I said and answered.

"Hello?"

"Is this Rebekka Franck?"

"This is she."

"This is Jack Ryder."

"Jack who?"

"Jack Ryder. Detective Jack Ryder. We ran into each other earlier today? The chimney case?"

This time I was really blushing. Not because he called, but because Sune had been right. I looked at him and he realized it too.

"Ha. I told you."

"What can I do for you, Detective?"

"I just wanted to call you and let you know that there

will be a funeral this coming Saturday. Maybe you'd like to attend? The mother, Jackie, asked me to let you know. She was very grateful for you being there."

"Sure. Sure. I'll be there. Thank you, Detective."

"No problem. See you Saturday, then."

I hung up. Sune gave me a look. He scoffed again, then shook his head. "I guess I can't blame you," he said. He grabbed his wheels and rolled his chair past me. "I'm not going to stand in your way anymore. You deserve to be happy. I'll move out once we get back home," he said and left the room.

23

"Mom, come out here!"

It was Julie. She was calling from the doorway. I wiped my tears away and got up from the bed. I walked out of the bedroom where I had been sitting the rest of the afternoon wondering what to do, worrying that things had completely broken between Sune and me. I wanted to talk to him, but I had no idea how to anymore. It didn't matter what I did or said, it was never good enough. I always ended up hurting him in some way. I thought about my ex, Peter, and how our marriage had ended so terribly and wondered if it had to do with me. Did I drive men nuts? Was I not cut out for relationships? I suddenly missed my dad and all his good advice. He would know what to say to make me feel better. He always did. Except, lately, he hadn't been talking much. Mostly sleeping a lot. He had a nurse working for him, bringing him food and feeding him and taking care of him so he wasn't alone, but still. I felt terrible for leaving him. What if he wasn't there when we got back?

"MO-OM!"

"I'm coming," I said and stepped out into the living room. I smiled to hide I had been crying. "What's going on?"

"Are you okay?"

Of course, she noticed. My daughter always did. No matter how much I tried to cover up that I was in a bad mood or sad, she always knew. She sensed it somehow.

"I'm fine," I said. "What's going on?"

"They're singing carols, Christmas carols, in our driveway."

"I love Christmas carols," I said and followed her outside, thinking this might cheer me up.

Sune was there with Tobias and William. William was in his lap, Tobias leaning on his chair. The choir sang beautifully, even though it was slightly strange to listen to Christmas carols in eighty-six-degree weather while cicadas were singing along in the background.

"*O holy night. The stars are brightly shining. It is the night of our dear Savior's birth.*"

Tobias was humming along next to me. He always was the musical one in our little family and actually had quite the voice. I had often encouraged him to sing for us, but he didn't want to. The first time I had heard his beautiful voice was once when he was in the shower and I walked past the bathroom, wondering who was in there. I listened for a little while, surprised at the power of this young boy's voice. But later, when I asked him to sing something for me, he refused to. Even in school, his music teacher had tried to get him to sing in the play, but he didn't want to. I had spoken to Sune about it and asked him if he thought we should give the boy vocal lessons, but Sune didn't think so.

"If the boy doesn't want to sing, then he shouldn't."

"But what if he just needs a little push, a little encouragement?"

But Sune had told me to leave it alone. Again, an issue where Sune and I were very different. If I discovered Julie had a talent, I would make sure to nurture it.

"Silent night. Holy night. All is calm, all is bright," they continued.

There were four adults and four children in the choir, but one little girl stood out to me. She was standing behind the other kids, a little to the left side, like she was hiding, like she—like Tobias—didn't like the exposure. But she was by far the best singer of them all. Her voice cut through all of them and made the rest of them fade in comparison. Especially when she, every now and then, closed her eyes and really let it out, not worrying about what everyone else was thinking; that was when she gave me goosebumps, even though it was eighty-six degrees and humid.

That was quite the accomplishment.

They sang *Jingle Bells* and we sang along, and then ended on *Ave Maria*, sung solo by the girl in the back. It was truly amazing and so magical it made me forget my troubles for a little while and kept me smiling for the rest of the evening.

24

Kristin was enjoying herself. So far, they had gone to most of the houses around the neighborhood, following their usual route, and all they had left was the nursing home.

Kristin stood in front of the old building, shivering slightly before entering. She never liked to go there since all those old people scared her with their wrinkled skin, toothless mouths, and skinny fingers pointing at her. Their nails were always long and cracked and yellow from smoking, their lips black from drinking coffee.

"Come on, Kristin," her mother said, carrying the cookies in a jar. She grabbed Kristin's hand and pulled her inside.

Even the smell was scary, Kristin thought. The smell of old lady mixed with death. It was the worst part of the tour. The only good thing was that when her mother passed out cookies to the old ladies, Kristin would usually get one also, and then if there were any more left once they got back out to the car, she would get another.

As usual, they walked from door to door at the nursing home. Many of the old people couldn't get out of bed, so the nurses opened all the doors to the rooms and the choir would stand in the hallway and sing. Some of the old folks would shut the door because they didn't want to hear the singing, Kristin's mother had explained.

"Some people get bitter and angry with age. Sometimes they just don't like Christmas."

Kristin didn't understand how anyone could dislike Christmas. What was there to not like? There was good food, pretty decorations, Christmas trees, presents, and then Santa. The merry man in the red suit who handed out presents. Who wouldn't love that?

"Hoo-oly night," she sang as the doors were opened. *"The stars are brightly shi-ning."*

An old woman peeked her head out the door, her long crooked fingers grabbing onto the wall, a toothless smile growing across her face. Kristin's mother stepped forward, offering her a cookie, and she accepted it. She took a bite, crumbs falling to the linolcum floor, some staying in the facial hair on her chin, wiggling as she chewed. She smiled widely and took another bite, crumbs staying on her black lips, which she was smacking loudly. She grinned at Kristin and Kristin could see the remains of the cookie on her tongue, wet and lumpy from her saliva, looking like dough. The old woman's pig-like eyes grew narrow as she squinted toward the carolers.

"Ding dong, merrily on high, In heaven the bells are

ringing," she sang, taking her eyes off the old woman, letting them settle on a man who was standing in the opening of his door, leaning on a cane, jacket on and a hat on his head like he was about to go somewhere. He looked like he was mad at them, maybe at the entire world, as he lifted his finger and pretended to be directing them, or maybe he was just moving his pointer finger to the rhythm of the song.

Another old woman entered from her room and started to sing along, her voice so loud and shrill it hurt Kristin's ears.

Kristin had to close her eyes to better focus, when she heard something coming from behind her and turned to look. She didn't see anything there, just a door that was ajar. But she was certain she had heard the sound of sleigh bells coming from behind it.

25

"Dashing through the snow."

Kristin was singing louder than ever to drown out the sound of bells ringing behind her. She kept looking over her shoulder, wondering who was there, who was behind the door jingling those bells.

"Oh, what fun it is to ride in a one-horse o-o-pen sleigh."

The jingling grew louder and louder until it was almost deafening to Kristin. She couldn't believe that none of the others in the choir were bothered by the loud jingling and turned around once again to look at the door. It was still ajar, but now there was something there. Someone was peeking out through the opening. It was no more than a crack and all she could see was a set of eyes. But, oh, what eyes they were. Glowing red like two Christmas globes in the light from a Christmas tree.

Santa?

TINKLE. TINKLE. TINKLE.

It almost sounded like he was talking to her through the sound of bells. She could see more of his face as she approached the door slowly, walking away from the choir. She could not only see his eyes, she could see the beard too, and the hat, the crimson red hat.

It is him. It is Santa!

Kristin couldn't control her eagerness. She walked to the door, listening only to the sound of the tinkling bells, wondering if Santa had come to give her presents or maybe even cookies. If there was one thing the two of them had in common, it was their love of cookies.

"*Oh, Jingle bells, jingle bells. Jingle a-ll the w-ay,*" the choir sang.

Kristin stopped and looked back at her mother, who was deeply immersed in the song she was singing, smiling and nodding at the old people, handing them cookies, letting them dig into the jar with their long skinny fingers and dirty nails. Kristin only hoped they wouldn't touch them all.

"Psst," Santa said from behind the door.

Kristin turned to look, but Santa was not there anymore. She couldn't see his eyes, but as she looked at it, the door swung open and Kristin approached it, happily.

"Santa?" she whispered and stood in the doorway.

"*The horse was lean and lank. Misfortune seemed his lot,*" the choir sang behind her, but Kristin was no longer listening.

"Santa? Are you in here?"

She took a step inside the room and scanned it in her search for the big-bellied man in his crimson suit. But there was no light in the room, and she couldn't see anything.

"Santa?"

The door slammed shut behind her. Kristin gasped and turned to look. Then she grabbed the handle to open it, turned it first one way, then the other, but it was locked. Desperately, she knocked on the door. She could still hear them singing on the other side.

"Jingle bells, Jingle bells, Jingle all the wa-a-ay..."

"Mom? Mom? MOM?"

But they didn't hear her, not her yelling or her knocking. Kristin heard movement behind her and turned to look in the sparse light coming in from under the door.

There he was. In all his might. His red eyes glowed in the darkness and lit up the room. He was holding his belly as he laughed, showing his pointy teeth behind the white beard, letting out that rumbling deep laugh Kristin used to cherish so much.

"Ho-ho-HO."

"S-Santa?"

He reached out his hand. There was something in it. Kristin stood on her tippy toes, then smiled, albeit cautiously, when she saw what it was.

"A cookie?"

"You want it?" he said.

She looked at the cookie in his gloved hand. It was the biggest cookie she had ever seen. It had big chocolate pieces in it the size of rocks. She looked up at him again, at his red glowing eyes and pointy teeth, then swallowed.

She nodded. "Can I?"

"Yeeesss," he said.

A sadness came over her face. "But...my mom says I can't have cookies because I'm trying to lose weight. To fit into my dress for my aunt's wedding this spring."

"Ho-Ho-Ho," Santa said like he found it amusing. "She's right, you know. If you're too fat, you might get stuck in the chimney. Can't have that happening, now can we?"

"I guess one little cookie can't harm me," Kristin said reaching out for it, thinking Santa seemed nice enough, even though he scared her a little at first.

Santa pulled the cookie away, then laughed loudly when he saw her disappointed face.

"Gotcha, didn't I?"

Kristin chuckled, slightly uncomfortable. She reached once again for the cookie and this time he let her have it. She grabbed the cookie between her fingers and pulled it toward her mouth, opening it widely. Santa was staring at her, eagerly watching her every move. Kristin could no longer hear the choir singing or the bells jingling as she plunged her teeth into the soft cookie and let the chocolate melt on her tongue. She closed her eyes and chewed, slowly letting the taste and pleasure spread throughout her body. It was the best cookie she had ever tasted. But why wouldn't it be? It was, after all, from Santa himself and if anyone knew about cookies, it had to be him.

Santa giggled and Kristin opened her eyes again, then smiled. "Thanks, Santa."

She turned to leave.

Santa grabbed her arm.

He held onto it so firmly, she couldn't move. Kristin tried to pull away, but Santa seized it, his face changing into something so terrible, Kristin couldn't even utter a word to explain it or scream out loud.

As he threw her out the window of the third-floor of the building, she could hear the choir singing *Joy to the World*.

Just before her face was smeared onto the pavement beneath, she couldn't help wondering who would sing her solo since she wasn't going to be there.

26

She didn't hear the thud as the body hit the ground outside because she was singing at the top of her lungs.

"Repeat the sounding joy, repeat the sounding j-o-y."

Patricia Walker was holding out the cookie jar to an old lady who was standing in her doorway while singing along loudly. She smiled at the woman as she took her cookie, then walked back, handing out one more cookie to each of their spectators. Many of the old folks had smiles on their faces, some were even singing along, joyfully, and that made it all worth it to Patricia. That was why she did it year after year. To spread the joy of Christmas around town.

She saved two cookies for her daughter and put a lid on the jar as they approached the end of the song.

"And wonders of his love, and wonders of his love, and w-o-o-onders of his love."

The song ended and all the inhabitants of the nursing

home clapped their hands and cheered. Patricia nodded and smiled, enjoying the applause. They had reached the last part of the show, the part she enjoyed the most. Kristin's solo. As a mother, she was naturally extremely proud of her daughter and she wished that Kristin enjoyed it more. She used to love singing in front of people, but ever since she had gained all the weight, and since that kid had commented on it during last year's caroling, pointing fingers at her while yelling all those ugly things, since then it had been harder to get her to perform in front of a crowd. And this year, she had insisted on hiding herself in the back behind the other kids, much to Patricia's sadness. She wanted her daughter to be proud of herself, of who she was, and especially of how well she sang.

"Now, we have one last song," she said. "The highlight of the show, at least for me personally. This is a solo performed by my own daughter, Kristin, singing *Ave Maria*. Kristin, take it away."

The crowd clapped, Patricia turned around to look for her daughter, but she wasn't there.

"Kristin?"

The choir stepped aside, but her spot was empty. Panic erupted inside of Patricia.

Easy now. Calm down. She probably just needed to go to the bathroom. She'll be right back.

"Kristin?"

Her voice was breaking, even though she tried hard to hide it. "Have any of you seen Kristin?" she asked the other members of the choir, which mostly consisted of friends and neighbors. They answered by shaking their heads.

"She was just here," Tracy, whom Patricia had known since high school, answered. "A minute ago."

The rest of them nodded in agreement. They were right, she couldn't have gone very far away; she had to still be at the nursing home. Somewhere. But where? Patricia started looking in the bathroom down the hall, but Kristin wasn't there.

"Kristin? Kristin? KRISTIN?"

No one had seen her. Patricia rushed through the hallway, yelling her name, opening all the doors and looking inside the old people's rooms, asking for her. Still, no one had seen her. Not that she trusted the old people's memory much or believed they would even remember if they had seen her, but even though she searched their rooms, she didn't find her.

Finally, she decided to walk outside to see if Kristin might have gone back to the car or maybe stood out on the stairwell to get some fresh air. Kristin had never liked singing at the nursing home much. Maybe it got to be too much for her this time.

Patricia ran through the lobby and opened the glass doors, pushing them forcefully open, calling her daughter's name.

"KRISTI-I-IN!"

The rest of the choir was right behind her and when she stopped at the bottom of the stairs, as soon as she saw the blood, they stopped too.

After that day, none of them ever sang a Christmas carol again.

27

"I can't believe it."

"What is it, Mommy?"

We were eating breakfast at the beach house. I was reading the local news on my iPad. Initially, I was actually looking for the opening hours to Kennedy Space Center since I wanted to take the kids there today, when I stumbled upon *Florida Today* and the article.

I put the iPad down and looked at Sune. "You remember the choir from last night?"

He hadn't spoken to me all morning, or even much the evening before other than small grunts and grumbles, so I don't know why I believed he would do so now. But he did. We had agreed to not let the kids feel anything and not let our fighting ruin their Christmas, so maybe that was why.

"Yes," he said. "What's with them?"

"One of the kids died last night."

"One of them died?" Julie said, speaking with a gasp

of fascination.

"She jumped out the window on the third floor of a nursing home," I said. "While they were there caroling for old people. Can you believe it?"

Sune shrugged. He gave me a look. "Maybe it isn't something we should talk about at breakfast. You know, with the kids listening and all. Just a suggestion."

But it was too late. Julie was already gobbling it all down, wanting to know more.

"What happened?"

"Suicide. They say she killed herself," I said.

Sune made a grimace for me to stop. I shrugged, signaling it was too late for that now.

"Wow. Who was it?"

I showed her the school picture of the girl from the article.

"I remember her," she said. "She was the one who could really sing, wasn't she?"

I nodded. "Yes. It's a shame. She was really good. And she was only eight years old. Can you imagine?" I felt a pinch in my stomach thinking about the mother. Surviving your own children had to be the worst fate for a mother to have to overcome. Especially to suicide. You'd have to wonder for the rest of your life, wouldn't you? *Could I have done anything to stop her? Why didn't I see it coming?*

Julie looked pensive. "Why would anyone kill themselves?"

I sighed. "Come here," I said and put her in my lap. She was getting a little too big for it, her long legs sticking out oddly, but I could still hold her. "They say here that she had been bullied because of recent weight gain. It says that she was upset and sad about it, so that's why they figure she jumped out the window."

"Wow. I could never do that."

I sipped my coffee, then looked at Sune. I knew he had had thoughts of suicide right after the doctors gave up on him the first time. He had told me about it and it had frankly terrified me. Was he still suicidal? If we split up, would he do it?

"I wanna go in the pool," Julie said and got off my lap.

"I'm coming too," Tobias yelled and ran off with her. I chuckled at how fast children's perspectives could change. They felt the sadness but didn't cling to it for long.

"I was thinking we could go to Kennedy Space Center today," I said, looking hopefully at Sune.

He shook his head. "Not today."

"Why not?"

He turned his back to me and rolled away, then stopped. "Don't you have that funeral to go to?"

"Sure, but..."

"We can't do both."

"I thought we could do it afterward," I said, but he was gone.

I could hear Julie and Tobias jumping in the pool, while William had found some puzzle game that he was trying to do, even though none of the pieces matched no matter how much he tried to force them to.

I decided Kennedy Space Center could wait.

28

THE CEREMONY WAS HELD at the local church, Club Zion. It was actually within walking distance from our beach house, so I decided to just walk over there on my own. There was no reason for anyone else in my family to attend. I only wanted to pay my respects to Jackie, the mother whom I felt a deep connection to after being with her in her darkest hour. It was something Sune had a hard time understanding, but so be it. I didn't need his permission, even though he thought I only went to see the detective.

I walked inside and spotted Jackie at the entrance, clinging onto her older daughter's shoulder, as if she would fall if she weren't there to support her. Next to her stood her husband, whom I also recognized from that fatal morning at their house. His face was stiff and stern and he seemed disconnected from the rest of his family like he had somehow been detached at some point and didn't know how to get back.

Jackie's eyes were filled with such a deep shock, I could hardly recognize her. I walked up to her and reached out my hand, offering my condolences the way everyone else did. When she saw it was me, she grabbed my hand and held onto it, as if she was afraid I might leave. She looked me in the eyes.

"Thank you, Rebekka. Thank you so much for coming."

I put my hand on her arm. She was hurting my other hand, holding onto it so tight. "I am so sorry," I said.

She pulled me into a hug that took me quite by surprise. I hugged her small fragile body, holding her tight until she let go of me on her own.

"He just loved Christmas so much," she said. "He wanted so badly to see Santa."

"I know," I said, even though I didn't. I didn't know anything about the kid or what he loved or didn't love. But it didn't matter.

Another guest arrived and Jackie let go of my hand, letting it linger in hers a little longer, like she really didn't want to let go of it, before finally attending to the new arrival. I snuck into the church, found a seat and sat down, feeling everything but comfortable.

Someone slipped in next to me. "I hate these things," he said.

It was the detective. Jack Ryder. I blushed and looked at him. "Who doesn't?" I said.

He nodded. "Good point."

"But, I agree. It's the worst when it is children."

We had been given a pamphlet when we entered

with pictures of Tobin inside of it and the lyrics to the songs we would be singing. I couldn't help noticing they were all Christmas songs, but according to what it said in the pamphlet, those were all his favorite songs just as Christmas had been his favorite time of the year. My guess was it would never be his family's.

I noticed Jack Ryder's wedding ring and it filled me with relief. Of course, a guy like that was married. Sune had been overreacting. He had called just because the mother had told him to. He wasn't interested in me at all.

"I heard there was another kid who died last night?" I asked.

Jack Ryder nodded with a deep sigh. "It's that time of year, I guess. For suicide, I mean. Last year, we had a psychiatrist kill himself. There's always a lot of craziness around Christmas."

"But Tobin wasn't a suicide?"

"No, that was a freak accident. The kid did something stupid. It happens, unfortunately. All we can do is pray it won't happen to one of our own, am I right?"

"Right."

The ceremony began and we were asked to stand up. I stood next to him, wondering about that craziness he said occurred around Christmas. Was that a universal thing or just here in Cocoa Beach?

29

It was such a beautiful ceremony. It made me cry. No, that's putting it too mildly. I was bawling my eyes out. I simply couldn't stand the thought of that poor woman losing her only son. It was too much to bear. Detective Ryder ended up holding me while I cried and I saw him shed a few tears himself as well. I have always admired a man who dares to cry.

"I am sorry for being such a mess," I said as we exited the church.

"That's okay," he said with a sniffle. "It was a tough one."

I had grabbed a Kleenex on my way out and blew my nose in it. "I never even met the kid," I said. "And look at me."

Ryder put his arm around me and chuckled. "Don't worry about it. I do that too. I was thin..."

He stopped and looked at something. I pulled away from him to see what he was looking at. It was a young girl, a few years older than Julie, but other than that she reminded me a lot of her, especially in the way she was looking at us with anger in her eyes.

"Sydney," Jack Ryder said.

The girl approached him.

"What are you doing here?" he asked.

"You know what I'm doing here," she said, speaking through gritted teeth. She handed him the pamphlet with Tobin's face on it. "Still think it was a suicide?"

"What are you talking about?" he asked.

"He didn't kill himself, just like Tobin's death wasn't an accident."

Ryder grabbed the girl's arm and pulled her away from the crowd. "Don't say stuff like that here. These people are in the middle of mourning the death of their son."

"The same death you claim is an accident. Who on earth is so stupid as to climb up into a chimney, huh?"

Sydney's face was glowing red now. I stood awkwardly beside them as they discussed it. Ryder was trying to keep his voice down, Sydney yelling as loud as she could, creating a scene.

"You need to go home now, Sydney," Ryder said and pulled her further away. "I am not letting you ruin this for the family."

He escorted her down the road where I saw him let go of her and point in the opposite direction, yelling at her to stay away or he'd have to call her mother. The kid then yelled something back at him before she started to walk away.

Jack Ryder returned, red in the face, and approached me.

"What was that about?"

He sighed and ran a hand through his blond hair. "The kid lost her dad last year and now she has all these theories. I feel bad for her, really. She has a hard time accepting that he's gone. I've tried to talk to her and explain things to her, but she won't listen. The kid has got these crazy ideas. I just can't let her ruin this moment for Tobin's family."

"Of course not," I said, looking in the direction of the girl who had started to walk down the street. I reached out my hand. "It was nice to meet you again, Detective. I need to get going. My family is waiting for me."

"Sure. Of course. Nice to met you again, Rebekka Franck."

I waved, then rushed after the girl and caught up with her halfway down Ninth Street.

30

We had coffee at Juice 'N Java. My treat. We found an empty area inside with some soft couches and sat down.

"So, tell me," I said after a few minutes of silence. "What was all that about today?"

She leaned forward. Her brown eyes lingered on me. She seemed to be a very smart girl; you could almost tell by the look in her eyes.

"Last year, my dad died in December. He hit a tree somewhere inland. They called it a suicide since there were no other cars on the road and since there were no signs that he tried to brake before hitting the tree. No marks on the asphalt. That's what they told us."

"But you don't believe them?"

"It doesn't add up. My dad had no reason to kill himself. Sure, he and Mom had their troubles, but who doesn't? There was no way he could have killed himself. He would never do that to my sister and me. He loved us so much. Too much to do something like this."

I shrugged. "That's what all people say when their loved ones kill themselves. It's fairly normal for it to feel like it came right out of the blue."

She shook her head and sipped her coffee. "There's more."

"I had a feeling there might be," I said and leaned forward on the soft couch. The café had a nice big-city look to it with modern art on the walls made by local artists, surfboards strapped under the ceiling, and the couches and armchairs upholstered in denim fabric. "You don't strike me as someone who would let this go easily."

"I have one question for you that I haven't seen answered in the case of Tobin," she said.

"And that is?"

"Who lit the fire in the fireplace? The mom and the dad and the sister all say they didn't do it. Either they're lying or something else is going on."

I nodded and sipped my coffee. "All right. You have my attention," I said. "Dazzle me."

"I think something is going on," she said, lowering her voice. "Something really odd. I don't have the specifics but there is a connection between these deaths and I've been looking into it. In 1992, a kid died on Christmas morning. Eight years later, Rob Wilson disappeared while walking with his girlfriend in Osteen Park. Both incidents happened in December, both cases were never solved. Last year, my dad died, and this year, Tobin. Too many unresolved incidents in the same month and if I keep looking, I'm sure I'll find more."

"But does anything else connect them except for the

fact they happened in December and were here in the Cocoa Beach area?" I asked.

She nodded. She grabbed her backpack and pulled out some printouts, then showed them to me, looking over her shoulder.

"What's this?" I asked and looked at the pictures.

"These are all from the police files. From their autopsies."

"And just how did you come upon them, might I ask?" I said, sounding a little more like a mother than what I cared for.

"You don't need to know that," she said. "I have my ways."

I smiled and sipped my coffee, thinking about Sune and how he used to have his ways of getting me any information I needed. I missed those days when we worked together.

"Okay, and what am I looking at?"

"All of them have these," she said and pointed at a set of small red marks on a man's neck. "All of them with no exception."

31

"In the reports, they always conclude it's some sort of bug bite. None of the forensics experts put a question mark on it or even realized the connection. They just conclude that it is a bug bite; some say it's a spider-bite, others that it's from a mosquito."

I was intrigued, to put it mildly. The girl was certainly onto something. I stared at the picture of Tobin's neck, what was left of it, and realized he had two marks that looked very fresh on his skin.

"And you say your dad had those too?" I asked.

She placed a picture in front of me. "Probably a bite from a spider or red ant, the forensics' report said."

"I'll be..." I looked at the pictures. They were all the same. I pointed at one, then asked: "Who is this?"

"Rob Wilson. Died in the year two thousand when walking with his girlfriend in the park. The body wasn't recovered until many years later. She was blamed for killing him, but once the body was found in a pond nearby years later, they couldn't prove she had done it even though they tried. But the body was very well preserved. The girl ended up in a mental institution. Years later, she was on trial for killing her husband, or ex-husband if you prefer. It was also her younger brother who was killed in December of 1992. Infant death syndrome, they said, but the kid was five. Rumors later had it that she killed him because she was jealous of him, but it was never proven. She was in the room when the parents entered and found him. That's how the rumors began. The kid had the same two marks, look."

"So, this woman had two people she cared about die like this?" I asked. "And you say she was on trial for killing her husband?"

"Ex-husband, yes. She shot him on Christmas morning. He came down the chimney and she thought he was Santa, she said. He was dressed like Santa and wanted to surprise their kid. He had recently left her, and the prosecutor argued she killed him because he had taken their daughter from her and wanted custody. The media called her the Santa-Shooter."

"Why would she shoot Santa?"

"I don't know. Here's where it gets really weird."

"Yes?"

"She was the last woman to see my dad alive."

I put my coffee down. "You're kidding me."

"Nope. He was evaluating her. He worked for the government from time to time to evaluate prisoners to see if they were fit for trial or not. He found her perfectly fit. When he left the prison, he ran into a tree without even trying to stop. When they did the autopsy, he had those two red marks on his neck just like the rest of them."

I leaned back on the couch, thoughts spinning like crazy inside of me. "I'll be..."

"I know."

"And no one wants to listen to you when you tell them about this, I take it?" I asked and looked at the pictures once more.

"You saw it with your own eyes today," she said. "As a matter of fact, you're the first one to ever listen to me."

I looked at Sydney, wondering about everything she had told me. It would be so easy for me right now to just walk away, to tell her I didn't believe any of what she told me, but something inside of me, an intuition, told me she was on to something. I knew I was on vacation but somewhere in there was a story buried and this girl needed it to be told. She needed it in order to be able to move on.

I pointed at the guy who had disappeared in the year two thousand. "I think the clue lies with this woman. It seems like she is connected to a lot of these deaths. I think we need to talk to her. What's her name?"

"Sara. Sara Andrews. She's on death row in a prison outside of Orlando."

32

We ordered an Uber to take Sydney home before I hurried back to the beach house. The kids were sitting in the living room, William and Tobias doing the puzzle while Julie was on the computer. Sune was sitting by the window looking at the ocean.

"I'm back," I said and kissed Julie on the top of her head.

I approached William and Tobias.

"Mommy!" William said, gnawing on his pacifier. It made me cringe. I was so ready to get rid of it.

"Let me take that for a second," I said and pulled it out of his mouth with a smile. "There. Now I can better hear what you're saying."

"Binky!" he cried, reaching out for it.

I shook my head. "No, you're a big boy now, remember? And big boys don't talk with something in their mouths."

"Binky!" William cried again, reaching for it. "Gimme."

"No. No. Remember what we talked about when we left on this trip? That it was time for you to give that thing up."

"BINKY!"

"Just give him the darn thing," Sune hissed from his spot by the window.

"No," I said as William's crying intensified. "He needs to get rid of it. He's four years old, Sune. It's ruining his speech and his teeth."

"He's just a kid. He'll be fine," Sune said.

"Gimme, gimme," William cried and reached out for the pacifier in my hand, tears streaming across his cheeks.

"He needs to get rid of it."

"Does it have to be right now? Just give it to him," Sune said again.

Will was inconsolable by now. All he could think about was the binky, and the crying grew stronger and louder. Finally, Sune had enough. He turned his chair toward me.

"Why did you have to come in here and ruin everything? We were having a nice, quiet time until you got here."

Ouch.

I threw out my arms with a deep sigh. "I can't do anything right by you, can I?"

The two big kids exchanged looks that obviously said, *Here we go again.*

Sune grumbled something, then rolled past me into the kitchen. "How was the funeral?"

"It was...tough."

I walked to the fridge and grabbed a bottle of water, then drank from it. "He was just a kid, Sune."

"Was he there?"

"Who? Detective Ryder? Yes, he was. This is a small community where people look out for one another and of course he was there to pay his respects like the rest of us."

"I wasn't asking for his entire story, just asking if he was there or not."

Sune grabbed a banana and peeled it. He was annoying me so much right now I could cry.

"Were you at the funeral all this time?"

I looked away. I didn't want to lie to him. "No. I went for a coffee at Juice 'N Java afterward."

"With him, I take it?"

"Will you stop with the jealousy?" I said defensively.

"So, it was with him," he concluded.

"You know what? I don't have to listen to this anymore. You're the one pushing me away, and I get it. I really get it, Sune. You're angry and bitter and sad and you have the right to be, but I can't keep doing this. I can't keep being your punching bag."

He looked into my eyes. I searched for softness in them but found none. Where was my beloved Sune? Where was the boy I had fallen in love with, the funny, crazy wonderfully irresponsible Sune who always made me laugh and always looked positively at things?

He smiled sarcastically. "Then, don't."

33

Next to the day that her brother died, this Saturday had to have been the worst day in Alyssa's entire life. Luckily, it was almost over, she thought to herself as she closed the door to her bedroom tightly, and finally let out the tears she hadn't dared to shed all day. She put her back against the door and slid to the floor, letting out a deep sigh. The days since her brother got stuck in the chimney had been like a nightmare that she couldn't wake up from. Her mother had broken down completely and could do nothing without Alyssa's help. She could barely even walk. Meanwhile, her father had completely shut down and barely uttered a word to any of them. Alyssa guessed he had to be in a state of shock of some sort. She had read a lot about it online in groups she followed about kids who lost a family member. She talked with a bunch of kids in there and asked for advice. She wouldn't know what to do without those kids to help her. They had no other family since all their grandparents had passed away and her mother was an only child. The only one they had left besides them was her uncle, her father's brother, but they hadn't spoken to each other since they had that argument over their inheritance after their parents' death. Alyssa couldn't understand how money could destroy something as deep as being brothers.

But that left Alyssa as the only one to take care of her parents. Who was going to take care of her?

Alyssa sniffled, then walked to her computer and sat down. She wrote to her friends in the group chat.

JUST BURIED MY BROTHER. WHAT A NIGHTMARE. MY PARENTS ARE A MESS. I DON'T KNOW WHAT TO DO. WILL IT EVER GET BETTER?

She leaned back in her chair, thinking about her brother and how badly she missed him already. He was a pain in the neck, but of course she loved him. She was his sister, for cryin' out loud.

She pulled out the desk drawer and pulled out a package of cigarettes. She walked to the window, opened it and lit one, blowing the smoke into the salty air coming from the ocean. She wondered if her mother would be able to smell it on her, smell that she had been smoking, then doubted she would even care.

It was dark outside now. She had told her parents she was going to bed, but they didn't even react. The house had been filled with people after the ceremony, people bringing food and tilting their heads, asking her mother how she was holding up.

No one asked Alyssa that same question.

Alyssa blew out smoke into the darkness. She didn't really like smoking that much, but it calmed her down. She killed the cigarette in an old can, then closed the window as she heard a sound indicating that someone had replied in the chat.

IT DOESN'T GET BETTER. BUT IT GETS EASIER TO LIVE WITH, someone wrote.

That wasn't much of an answer.

Alyssa sighed. She could hear her parents coming up the stairs now and they'd be getting ready for bed. Alyssa looked at her own bed and questioned whether she would be able to sleep at all after this day.

SO THAT'S IT? I JUST HAVE TO LIVE WITH IT? THIS IS MY LIFE NOW?

She wrote, tears piling up in her eyes. She didn't know how to live with this pain inside of her, with this somber darkness that had fallen upon her childhood home. She wanted it to go away. She wanted to wake up from this freakin' nightmare.

34

Alyssa fell asleep at her desk and woke with a gasp. Disoriented, she looked at the clock on the computer. It was past midnight. Her head was hurting from sleeping like that and she felt groggy.

Many of her friends had written in the chat, trying to cheer her up, but she didn't want to read what they said. It didn't make her feel any better anyway. Nothing did.

Alyssa's stomach growled and she remembered that she hadn't eaten all day, even though the house had been filled with food carried in by all the friends and neighbors who had been at the ceremony and had come to the house afterward to pay their respects. There had to be at least fifteen lasagnas still somewhere down in the kitchen.

Alyssa got up and walked out in the hallway, walking cautiously to not wake up her parents. As she passed Tobin's door, she paused. The door was ajar and, for just a second, it was like he wasn't gone. Like none of this had happened. She imagined him in there in his bed, sleeping, or maybe sitting at his desk, drawing under the light of his lamp. Alyssa poked the door and it opened up a little more so she could see inside. She peeked in, but of course, Tobin wasn't in his bed or sitting at his desk. Of course not. It hadn't all been a dream or some freakish nightmare.

It doesn't get better. Just easier to live with.

Alyssa sighed and walked down the stairs into the kitchen. She found a bunch of the lasagnas stabled on the counter. The rest were packed in the refrigerator and in the freezer. The ones left out were the ones that there was no room for.

Couldn't people think of any other dish to bring? Alyssa couldn't stand lasagna and after this was over, she was never going to eat the dish again.

It's not gonna be over, Alyssa. Only easier to live with.

She grabbed a plate and cut herself a piece, then sat down at the breakfast counter and ate. It didn't taste like anything. No food had tasted good since her brother died. It all tasted like that awful smell that had been in their house on the morning they found him. The same smell the entire house still reeked from.

The stench of burnt skin.

They believe he had still been alive, the police had told them. That Tobin had gotten stuck and maybe passed out inside the chimney and then when the fire was lit, he had been suffocated by the smoke and his body burned. About-two thirds of it was completely charcoaled while the head and shoulders remained untouched.

Alyssa shivered when thinking about it, and lost her appetite. She put the plate in the sink, then grabbed a glass of water and drank. As she swallowed the cold water, she thought she heard the sound of bells ringing, but shook it off as being ridiculous. When she put the glass down, it was there again, sounding even closer.

It's probably coming from the road outside. Maybe someone is walking their dog with bells on the leash or collar.

Alyssa spotted a box of chocolates and opened it. She unwrapped a piece and ate it when she heard the jingling again. This time, it sounded just like it came from the living room. She walked in there.

"Hello?"

Nothing.

Alyssa shook her head and was about to walk away when she heard the jingling again. She gasped and turned around, realizing it was coming from the chimney.

What the heck?

"Hello? Who's there?"

Still nothing.

Alyssa sighed and walked back toward the kitchen to grab another glass of water. The chocolate had made her thirsty. It always did. She had almost reached the end of the carpet when she stopped. There it was again. The sound of darn jingle bells.

"Hello?"

Alyssa turned around and faced the chimney. Was this some sort of sick joke? Was someone playing a trick on her?

"Who's there?"

A dripping sound caught her attention. Alyssa held her breath as she spotted the blood dripping from inside the chimney into the fireplace. She gasped and backed up, then turned around to run, when she stopped. In front of her stood her brother. He was holding a plate of cookies in one hand and a glass of milk in the other.

"T-Tobin?"

But it wasn't really Tobin. Looking into his eyes, she knew it wasn't. His eyes were dead. His lips were colorless, the skin on his face grey. He held out the plate of cookies toward her.

"Christmas is my fa-a-vo-rite time of year," he said. "What's your fa-a-vo-rite time of year, Alyssa?"

Alyssa stumbled backward with a loud whimper. Tobin remained still, staring at her with his soft brown—yet lifeless—eyes. She was paralyzed until the boy's mouth turned upward in a slow steady smile and showed off a set of very sharp teeth and soon wasn't a boy anymore, but a man, a grown twinkly-eyed man with red gleaming cheeks wearing a crimson red suit and a black belt holding in his plump stomach.

"S-Santa?"

Santa bent forward. He hissed at her and snapped his teeth, his breath smelling like candy canes and cookie dough. Alyssa stormed past him up to her room, slammed the door shut, blocked it with her chair, and pulled the covers over her head.

As she lay there the rest of the night, wondering if she was going insane, she was certain she could still hear Santa's deep jovial laughter coming from downstairs.

PART III

35

Sara Andrews—aka the Santa-Shooter—was small and skinny. If she had been beautiful, it was a long time ago. She was younger than me but looked like she could easily be ten years older.

I had come as a reporter and told the prison I was here to ask her to tell me her story for an article. It wasn't completely a lie since I would write a story about the strange deaths in Cocoa Beach if there was a story there. I just didn't know who I would write it for. I doubted Jens-Ole would put it in our local paper back home since the people dying weren't Danish, but as the days passed, I got the idea that maybe I could sell the story to a newspaper over here and make a little money while on vacation. We sure could use it.

Assuming there was a story to tell.

Four days had passed since the funeral and things had gotten better at the house. Sune was still angry with me and at the world, but the kids and I had started to really enjoy our little vacation here in paradise. I was beginning to look forward to spending Christmas in the beach house and we had even bought a tree. It felt weird that it was so warm when carrying the tree inside and decorating it, but somehow, I enjoyed the change it provided. This was so different from any other Christmas we had ever experienced, and to me, it was quite exotic.

The kids had been begging to go to Disney World soon and I had promised them we would. So far, we had been to Kennedy Space Center, which I found very interesting and so did the boys, whereas Julie found it boring and kept asking where the rides were. Somehow, she had gotten it into her head that it was like an amusement park and there would be roller-coasters and not just boring old rockets and old spacesuits worn by people so long ago she couldn't even imagine it.

Those were her words, not mine.

"I'm Rebekka Franck," I said and shook Sara's hand when she approached me flanked by two prison guards.

We sat down. The guards retreated to the wall behind them. I smiled compassionately, yet a little anxiously. The woman was—for all I knew—a murderer. She had killed her ex-husband and maybe also her boyfriend and younger brother.

"So, you're a reporter, huh?"

"Yes."

"From Denmark?" Sara scoffed. "Am I really so interesting that they'd send some reporter all the way from across the pond?"

I nodded. "Well, I was here anyway, but I stumbled across your story by accident and wanted to tell it."

"What story?"

"That's what I was hoping you'd tell me."

I reached into my backpack and pulled out a file of papers. Sydney had helped me get ahold of some things from her dad's stuff. Among them, a notepad, the one he had used to take notes when interviewing Sara Andrews. I flipped through the pages, then stopped at one, and showed it to her.

"Last year about this time, you were evaluated by a psychiatrist."

"Dr. Hahn, yes. He didn't believe a word I said."

"You do know he is dead now, right?"

Sara froze. Her big eyes stared at me. "No, I didn't."

"He hit a tree with his car right after talking to you. They called it suicide, but his daughter is of another opinion. You were the last person to speak to him."

Sara rubbed her face. "I'll be..."

I showed her the picture of Dr. Hahn's neck that Sydney had given me. "He had these red marks," I said and watched her reaction. It was violent. Her shoulders were shivering. Her eyes reached mine.

"I thought you might recognize them?"

"I...I..."

She didn't say any more, only shook her head like she didn't believe what she had seen.

"The last thing Dr. Hahn wrote on his notepad when he spoke with you was," I continued, while reading up from the notepad: "SANTA, AN

ANAGRAM FOR SATAN, followed by a question mark."

I paused and looked into her eyes again.

"Now, why would he write that?"

36

Sara Andrews wasn't speaking at all. She was simply staring at me, her eyes wide and fearful.

"When I read the notes, it seems that you kept mentioning Santa," I said. "Like here, when you speak about your younger brother who was killed back in '92, and your boyfriend when he disappeared, you told Dr. Hahn it was Santa who killed them, am I right? Was that why you were ready to shoot your ex-husband when he came down the chimney? Because you believed Santa was coming?"

Sara Andrews shook her head. "I...I don't..."

She stopped. I could tell I was losing her. Tears sprang to her eyes. "I've spent so much time trying to forget," she said. "Telling myself it wasn't true, that I made it up. I can't...I can't go back there."

I looked at her, scrutinizing her. I didn't know what to think. Up until now, I had believed she was nuts, paranoid even, thinking Santa somehow was out to get her, but she didn't seem to be. I was still hoping she could give me something to move on.

"So, what you're saying is you made up the part about Santa?" I asked.

Sara still shook her head. Her eyes became distant. "No. No. I can't...I can't talk about it."

"Why not?"

Her eyes met mine, yet they still seemed far away.

"Because I don't know. I don't know what happened. All I know is I saw him. I saw him in my brother's bedroom on the night he died, blood dripping from his teeth. The teeth that left that mark, the same as in that picture there on my brother's neck. I also saw him come out from between the trees in the park and attack Rob, who got so happy when he saw Santa that he ran to him. He used his...long pointy nails to rip open his vein, the one in his throat, the big one, and blood...blood was everywhere. I saw him, but I don't know if he was real. They tell me he wasn't. For years, that's what they have told me. That I made him up because of all the awful things I had done. That he was only in my head. That I made him up because I couldn't face my own actions. Every time I talk about it, bad things happen. Like me shooting John. I can't let this happen to me again or to anyone else."

I bit my lip, trying to make sense of her and what she was telling me. I didn't know what I had expected from her, maybe a crazy bat crying loudly about Santa coming after her and wanting her dead, like the ones you'd meet in the subway. I knew she had blamed both deaths on

Santa, as I had researched her trial in the local newspapers since they seemed to have a blast telling the story of the crazy lady blaming sweet jolly Santa for killing her brother and boyfriend. Heck, I even found it funny when reading it, but now I didn't find it as amusing anymore.

I closed the notepad, wondering where I was even going with this. These deaths were all coincidences happening around December. It was just as detective Ryder had said. Christmas brought out all the craziness.

"I am sorry," I said. "Maybe this was a mistake."

Sara stopped me.

"Wait. You're the first one to ever listen to me when I spoke about these things," she said. "Most people only laugh at me."

"Well, can you blame them?" I asked.

She shook her head. "No. I would laugh too. Only I'm the one it happened to, so I'm not laughing anymore. I'll tell you my story, in detail, but the thing is, once I do, he might come after you too."

"Why do you say that?"

"Because you'll start believing in him. He only comes to those who believe."

I chuckled. "I'll take that chance."

37

I LEFT the prison feeling strange. I passed the tree where Dr. Hahn had been killed and recognized it from the photo in the police file. A chill ran down my spine when thinking about it and I accelerated, thinking about the stories I had just heard from this woman.

I didn't believe a word of it since it seemed so far out; I had to stop myself from laughing while she spoke. How could anyone believe something that ridiculous? Santa as a bloodthirsty entity?

But I didn't doubt for a second that Sara believed it herself. She had seen it and this was her story. I didn't know whether it brought me any closer to the real story, though, and I wondered about it as I drove back.

There had to be an explanation for all this. There simply had to be. I wanted to find it and hand it to Sydney, so she could finally move on. Maybe it was for my own sake as well. Because I couldn't stop thinking about Jackie and her son in the chimney. I needed some closure as well. I needed to answer one simple question:

Who started the fire?

As I found the beach-line and drove toward Cocoa Beach, I speculated whether there was some smart killer on the loose, someone good enough to cover everything up, to make it all look like accidents. One who had been active for twenty-five years?

But what about the marks, Rebekka? There were red marks on all of them.

I shivered and decided I didn't want to think about it anymore, then turned up the radio, found a good song, and sang along. I reminded myself I was actually on vacation and maybe I should just let it go for now. There really wasn't much of a story, if you looked at it, and maybe I should focus more on my family instead. I realized as I reached Cape Canaveral and A1A, that maybe I had only thrown myself into this story because I didn't know what to do about Sune and me. To give myself an excuse to get away. Maybe it was because I didn't want to face the real issue here, which was that I was sick of the situation with Sune but saw no way out. There was nothing I could do to make things better. I couldn't make him walk and he wouldn't even talk about it anymore.

I was fed up.

But what kind of woman leaves a loved one when they end up in a wheelchair? I had promised myself I wasn't going to do that. The fact was, I wasn't going to leave him because he was in a wheelchair, but because of the way he treated me, the way he had become. But in my mind, it would always be because of the chair, because of the accident. I would end up always feeling guilty about him.

I sighed and drove into downtown Cocoa Beach, which had to be the smallest downtown I had ever seen. It was cute, though, and I really liked it here. People seemed to be so happy and always polite and friendly.

I drove through town and into the driveway of the beach house and stopped the engine. Sune had been angry at me for leaving them again, but I was getting used to him disapproving of everything I did. It didn't matter what it was, so I had left anyway. I needed the excuse to get away. I needed a time-out. But the problem was, it hadn't helped anything. I still dreaded walking through that front door.

38

Sara Andrews was about to cry. When they escorted her back to her cell, she could barely keep it together. So many memories bubbling up inside of her, most of them terrifying. For so long, she had tried to not think about it; for so long, she had kept it away. Yet, here she was once again, wrapped up in the whole thing, unable to keep all those emotions and the fear away.

She was put inside the cell, the door shut and locked behind her. Left alone once again to her own thoughts.

Talking to the journalist had made it all come back, even though she had fought it, and now she could no longer keep it at bay. She kept seeing her baby brother through her inner eye, all pale and lifeless, the big Santa figure bent over him, his teeth covered in the poor boy's blood.

At night, she would often dream about it and, this night, as she dozed off, she did so again. She was back at her childhood home, waking up to the sound of jingle bells sounding from outside her room. Wondering if it was Santa bringing her presents, she rushed out into the hallway, then realized the sound came from her baby brother's nursery.

The door was ajar and Sara pushed it gently open, only to see the big man in the red suit. She had screamed loudly once she had grasped the situation, and Santa had disappeared. But it was already too late. Her brother was dead.

"Sara!" someone called and she woke up with a gasp, emotions overwhelming her as she once again realized her life had been nothing but one long nightmare.

She still remembered her mother's expression when she entered the room on that night. The look she had given Sara afterward. That was when she realized her mother blamed her for her brother's death. She believed Sara had somehow killed him. And after that, she had been terrified of her. Terrified of her own daughter.

Sara sobbed and wiped away tears as she sat on her bed in the darkness. So many things she regretted today, but how could she have acted differently? She had told Rob to not go near Santa, but he wouldn't listen. She had told John not to take their daughter to the mall to sit on Santa's lap. But he wouldn't listen either. And then when he came down that chimney, she had been certain it was him, the real Santa coming for her or even worse, her daughter, and she had shot him.

Poor John. Poor, poor John.

Sara leaned back on the bed that squeaked on its hinges, sounding like it was complaining. She couldn't find rest again and was tossing and turning when she heard a sound that made her blood freeze.

The tinkling sound of jingle bells.

Sara shot up in the bed. "Who's there?"

No answer.

"Who's there," she said, wondering why she would ask such a ridiculous question. Who could be there? She was inside a prison cell for cryin' out loud.

It's the hallucinations, Sara. Don't give into them. That's how the crazy starts.

TINKLE. TINKLE.

Sara stared into the darkness, her heart thumping in her chest.

TINKLE. TINKLE. TINKLE.

Slowly, she looked over the side of the bed and peeked under it. A set of glowing red Christmas globes looked back at her. A bearded face appeared as he came closer to hers, his breath smelling like candy.

"Have you been a good girl this year, Sara?"

A jolly laugh followed before he reached his long nails up toward her and grabbed her throat.

39

THE CHRISTMAS TREE in our living room was gorgeous. I enjoyed looking at it while baking cookies the next day. I was beginning to get my Christmas groove on and seriously looking forward to the big holiday.

The cookies smelled wonderful in the oven as I made a snack for Julie, who had gotten hungry between computer games. I hadn't seen Sune all morning or night either since he was sleeping on the couch in the media room and hadn't come out yet. I wondered if he would at all. He had to get hungry at some point, right?

"So, what are we doing today?" Julie asked.

William was still decorating the tree with some of the ornaments we had brought from home. He dropped a globe but luckily it was shatterproof and bounced right back up, much to his surprise and joy.

I shrugged. "I just want to hang out here and get a little Christmassy. How about you?"

"I think we need to go Christmas shopping soon," she said. "I haven't even bought one present."

She had a point. I had postponed the shopping because I really didn't enjoy it much, but it had to be done. And maybe it would be different now that we were over here. I had promised the kids to find a mall and take them shopping.

"Let's see," I said. "Maybe later today. Or maybe tomorrow, huh? There's always tomorrow."

"You keep saying that and you're gonna have a lot of crying faces come Christmas time," she said as she grabbed her sandwich and disappeared. Back to the computer, I guessed.

I sighed and looked at the cookies in the oven. Julie was right. We had to get some shopping done soon. I just didn't know what to say to Sune. Would he come with us? Play happy family? I had a feeling he wouldn't.

I sat at my laptop and went back to my research. I had been going through the town's history around Christmas and found at least five more deaths that they had no explanation for. And these were earlier. Five to six years earlier than when Sara's brother died. It couldn't have been her since she would have been an infant at the time. I kept searching and found a death dated back almost fifty years ago. December 1970. It caught my attention since it was a kid who had crawled up inside the chimney and gotten stuck. And not only that. Someone had lit a fire in the fireplace before they found him. But no one knew who had lit it. No one in the household would say they had done it. The old article said that they believed the father had done it, but wouldn't admit it.

I almost dropped the cup of coffee between my hands. This was almost fifty years ago. If this was some killer, then how was he also active back then?

"Cookies done?" William came up to me and said, pulling my jeans.

I laughed and grabbed him. I put him in my lap then kissed him, gently pulling the pacifier out of his mouth.

"When the oven goes DING, that's when cookies are done," I said and hugged him tightly.

"Say, DING," he yelled. "Say, DING!"

I chuckled and kissed him again, wondering what his life was going to be like if Sune and I decided to split up once we got home. Would Sune want to be a weekend dad at all? Or was he just so bitter and angry at the world and at all of us that he wouldn't even want to see his son? And what about Tobias? Would he take care of him alone and take him away from me? I had grown to love Tobias like he was my own. I couldn't stand the thought of not having him with me anymore.

Was Sune really going to rip us all apart?

I looked at the beautiful tree that William had helped decorate. It was a little heavy on one side with the ornaments, and on the bottom, since Will couldn't reach very high, but it was perfect. Just the way I liked it.

As I stared at the tree, I thought I saw a light in between the branches. A red glowing light. Actually, there were two of them. Like two red glowing Christmas globes staring at me.

I put William down and walked closer, but after two steps, the oven sounded, DING. William shrieked with excitement and I rushed to get the cookies out. As I took the plate out and looked at the tree again, the lights were gone.

40

We stayed at the house all day. It felt good to just hang with my kids and not have to go anywhere. We didn't even go down to the beach, but we did go in the pool for an hour or so before we returned inside the house to the freshly baked cookies and hot chocolate.

Sune stayed in the media room all day, probably sulking. I tried not to think about him while spoiling the kids with marshmallows in the hot chocolate and seconds on the cookies. I refused to let him ruin my vacation. The kids and I had been looking forward to this trip for ages and talked about how great it was going to be, and it had been crazy expensive, so I was determined to have a good time no matter what.

I knew Sune was disappointed and he was right to be. I, for one, didn't know how I would feel if it was me, to have been looking so much forward to seeing this doctor, hoping, praying he could heal you and then just being told that it was all in your head and that he couldn't help you unless you made some improvement first.

What a nerve that doctor had.

I was so furious at him I considered leaving a bad review on his webpage, but what was the use? I wasn't angry with him. I was mad at the entire situation, and so was Sune.

"We should have a fire in the fireplace," Tobias suddenly said.

We were sitting in the living room, spread out on the couches, drinking our hot chocolate. Julie and William were playing some card game that Julie obviously wasn't much into since she was constantly checking her phone, while William cheated.

I looked at the fireplace in front of us, then shivered. Ever since seeing that boy pulled out of the chimney, I wasn't too fond of the idea.

"Maybe another time," I said.

"Why not now?" Julie asked, finally looking up from her phone.

"Are you kidding me? It's like eighty degrees outside," I said.

"We can just crank up the AC," she said. "Make it feel like it's cold and wintery and Christmassy. Please, Mom?"

"Yes, please, Mom?" Tobias said.

I looked at him. He had never called me mom before. My heart sank thinking about how well we were doing as a family and how I was scared to lose it all again.

"No," I said. "I don't even know how to..."

"We could roast marshmallows," Julie said.

"Yeah!" Tobias said.

"Yeah," William repeated while sending me a look —*that* look—the one he knew I couldn't say no to, chewing aggressively on his pacifier. I sighed. Three sets of adorable eyes were staring back at me.

"I saw some firewood in the garage," Tobias said. "I can help you. I learned how to make a fire at boy scouts."

"Really?" I asked.

"Really," they all three repeated in unison, even though William's came a little later.

I smiled and shook my head.

"I'll get the firewood," Julie said and got up, leaving her phone on the couch.

"I'll look for a lighter," Tobias said. "I saw one on the grill outside."

"I'll get marshmallows," William said and stood up.

"You're really determined about this, huh?"

"Yes!" they all repeated in unison once again.

"All right." I chuckled while sipping my chocolate. I knew when I was outnumbered. "Guess we're having a fire then."

41

I turned the AC up and soon a cold wind blew from it, cooling the entire living room down. I found a blanket to cover up with while the kids brought everything in.

Tobias and Julie put the wood in place and then handed me the lighter. I walked to the fireplace and checked that the damper was open. I lit the lighter and checked that the draft went upward, then crumpled a few pieces of an old newspaper and put it as a foundation, then stacked the larger logs on top of it. I then lit the newspapers. The fire caught the papers fast. It smoked a little and I coughed, but seconds later, the fire had grabbed onto one of the logs and set it on fire.

"There we go," I said satisfied and pulled back.

"When can we do the marshmallows?" Julie asked. "I found some pointy sticks in the back that we can use."

"Just wait a little bit," I said. "Let the fire really get going."

I sat back on the couch and looked at the growing fire.

I had forgotten how much I loved having a fireplace. I used to have one when living with my ex-husband, Peter, and we would always light it around Christmas and a lot during the long cold winters.

I looked at Julie and wondered if she remembered that; I pondered how much she remembered of her father and her early childhood. Did she ever think of him? Did she miss him? We never talked about him anymore.

That kid had been through so much.

Damn you, Sune. We can't let it end like this. We can work it out, can't we? We always do. What happened?

The accident happened. He was shot in the stomach and the bullet went through his spine. That's what happened. Nothing had been normal ever since. It was two years ago now and Sune seemed changed forever; he was never really his old self anymore.

"It's dying," Julie said disappointedly.

"What's that?" I asked distraughtly.

She was sitting with the stick between her legs, the marshmallow already placed at the end of it.

"It's dying, Mom, the fire."

I looked at the fireplace. She was right. The fire was dying out. "That's odd," I said and got up. I found some more newspaper, crumpled it, and put it in there, then lit it. The fire flared up, but then something dripped down on it, causing the fire to die out.

"What the...?"

"What's happening, Mom?" Julie said and came closer.

I looked at the newspaper and realized it was soaked

in something and so was the firewood. Something that was dripping down from inside the chimney.

"Is that...Is that...?" Julie approached it, then let out a loud, bone-piercing scream.

I stared at the firewood as blood dripped down from the chimney, soaking everything. The kids were screaming behind me, terrified.

The door to the media room opened and Sune rolled inside. My heart was pounding in my chest as I backed up, staring at the blood raining down into the fireplace.

"What's going on here?" Sune asked. "Why is everyone screaming?"

"There's blood, Dad," Tobias shrieked. "B-blood in the fireplace."

Sune approached us, grumbling something, then looked at the fireplace and up at the chimney.

"I don't see anything."

"It's right there, Dad. Look."

Sune shook his head. "Must be an animal," he said, rolling away. "Probably a bird or maybe a raccoon that got stuck in the chimney. I'll call for a chimneysweeper. Don't just stand there, Rebekka. Get the kids out of the living room if a little blood scares them so much."

42

I took the kids to the yard and told them to play some soccer. I sat in a patio chair, feeling very unsettled, especially after seeing that kid pulled out of the chimney just a little further down the road.

It took maybe an hour or so before the chimneysweeper came. We told him what we had seen and he agreed with Sune; it was probably some animal that had gotten stuck.

"I couldn't see anything, but they all claim they saw it," Sune said.

"I'll get it out," the sweeper said, then he climbed onto the roof.

The kids weren't really playing, just staring at the chimney, eyes struck with fear.

"Don't worry, kids," I said. "I'm sure Sune is right. It's just some animal. There's nothing to be afraid of."

"But..." Julie said. "You saw that kid...what if..."

"Don't go there," I stopped her. "Don't even think it. It's not the same. Not at all."

The kids didn't seem to believe me. They kept staring at the chimney that the guy had now disappeared into.

"How about an ice-cream, huh?" I asked.

"Yay!" William said.

The two others didn't say anything. Still, I walked to the kitchen and grabbed a couple of cones that I had bought and closed the freezer again. I turned and, as I did, I was certain I heard something. It was coming from the corner where we had placed the Christmas tree. It sounded almost like the jingling of a bell. I walked closer to the tree, staring at it, wondering about the glowing red globes I had seen earlier.

"Is someone there?"

I could hear the chimneysweeper inside the chimney and shook my head. It was probably just him that I had heard. Maybe he had bells on his clothes or something. I turned around to walk back out when I heard a rustle behind me. I turned and looked at the Christmas tree.

Was it moving?

It was. The entire tree was shaking, all the lights on it suddenly turned on. I shrieked and pulled back. Then I saw something that made me look closer. In one of the globes, there was something, as a matter of fact, it was in all of them. Something was emerging inside of them, like a reflection, but it couldn't be. All of them showed the reflection of Santa. He was laughing, grinning from ear to ear, showing off a set of pointy teeth. I could have sworn I also heard him laugh.

Thinking he had to be right behind me, I turned to look, but no one was there, and as I turned back, the picture was gone and the lights had gone out. The tree was back to normal.

Heart pounding in my chest, I backed out of the living room, keeping my eyes on the tree, then rushed out to the kids and handed them each an ice cream.

"Are you all right, Mom?" Julie asked. "You're sweating."

I wiped my forehead. "Yeah, well...it's hot."

They ate their ice cream while I kept looking in through the window of the living room to see if the tree was still in place. It was.

About an hour later, the chimneysweeper came back down, shrugging. "I couldn't find anything. The chimney is as clean as it can be. Nothing is stuck in there. I went through it twice."

"But...but...what...about...?"

He shrugged again. "I don't know what to say to you. There's nothing there. Not even blood."

I thanked the guy, then looked at the kids. They all had terror in their eyes. No one was moving. Not even William. He was holding the ball between his hands, sucking his pacifier like that kid on *The Simpsons* while staring up at the chimney. Julie and Tobias were holding each other's hands, also looking up, then back at me.

"Mom?" Julie said.

I clapped my hands and smiled. "How about some Christmas shopping?" I had to get them to think about something else and to get us all out of this house for a little while.

"Let's go to the mall."

43

Merritt Island Square Mall was packed with people. Sune didn't want to come, so we left him back at the house. He had been on my case about the chimney and what we had seen, accusing me of spreading unnecessary fear among the kids, telling me I was hysterical and I had made the kids just like me. He didn't believe there had been blood and even when I showed him the bloody newspapers, he told me he couldn't see it.

"It's completely dry," he said. "It all looks perfectly fine to me."

I was glad that the kids had seen what I saw; otherwise, I would have thought I had gone crazy. I was starting to believe I was crazy, with the things I was seeing and hearing. Sune, on the other hand, believed I was making up stories and getting the kids to believe them.

"They'll believe anything you say."

"But it was there, Sune. The blood was there."

"I don't care what you tell yourself, just don't make the kids believe in it as well, okay?" he had ended the conversation and rolled back into the media room and slammed the door.

Now we were standing outside Macy's. Julie wanted to look for presents for me, so I let her go in on her own while the rest of us waited outside. Tobias wanted to go to the skate shop afterward and buy a cap for his dad. Meanwhile, William was being a pain in the neck. He had all this built-up energy and I could hardly keep him still. He kept disappearing into stores, where I had to go in and get him.

A big sign showing a picture of Santa had his attention now.

"Santa," he chirped, pushing the pacifier to the side of his mouth. I felt like all the other people in the mall were staring at him because of the stupid pacifier, thinking he was way too old to be using one. He was, but he was also a tall boy, so he looked a lot older than he was. I decided I didn't have to care what people thought.

"Yes, William, that's Santa," I said. I looked at the sign with him. It said Santa would appear on stage in the mall at two o'clock.

"Wanna see Santa," William said.

"No, William, not today, baby. Mommy is tired and I don't want to be in a line with a thousand people."

"See Santa," William said again, this time more determined.

"Not today," I said.

"Santa!" now he was stomping his feet.

"No," I said, grabbing him by the hand. "There's Julie now. Say, hi, Ju-Ju," I said and waved to get his attention on something else.

William pulled his hand out of mine, then yelled so loud it made everyone stop and stare:

"SANTA!"

Then he turned around and ran away from me as fast as he could.

"William! William! WILLIAM!"

It amazed me how fast this child could run when he really wanted to. People were staring wildly, some even grumbling things I didn't hear, and I worried that they thought I was some creepy child abductor trying to catch my next prey, but I had to stop him before he got lost.

I didn't catch up to him before he reached the food court, where he stopped in front of the big stage. Hundreds of kids were already in line.

William pointed at the stage, then said:

"Santa."

I sighed and grabbed him. "Yes, I know it's Santa, but we don't have time today, okay, buddy? Maybe next time."

William's expression grew angry. He pulled out his pacifier, then reached it toward the stage. "Binky."

"Ah, now I see. You want to give Santa your binky, just like we talked about. Of course." I sighed as Tobias and Julie caught up with us. "Well, I guess I can't say no to that, then. Let's get in line."

44

Sydney saw her own reflection in the window at Bath & Body Works. She looked pale. No wonder, with her being up all night most nights. She sighed and waited for her sister, who was touching everything in the store. They were looking for a present for their mother. She had told them that morning that she wanted a normal Christmas this year, as normal as it could be given the circumstances and their father not being there. Still, she was ready to move on.

"Life has to go on, right?" she said. "Besides, my girls deserve a good Christmas this year."

Sydney's' younger sister, Trisha, had beamed with happiness and so had Sydney. They had then decided to bike to the mall and start buying presents. So far, they had been everywhere, Macy's, Sears, Dillard's and still they hadn't found the right thing for their mother. Trisha had found many things she believed would be excellent presents, but Sydney wanted it to be perfect. This year was going to be absolutely perfect. Sydney knew her mother didn't have much strength to arrange everything, so she would take it upon herself to do whatever she couldn't. All Sydney wanted was to give her baby sister a real Christmas. She deserved it. This year had been tough on her.

"Let's go in here," Sydney said and pointed at JC Penney. Once inside, she grabbed a dress and pulled it out into the light. She held it up and tried to picture her mother wearing it.

"You think she would like this one?" she asked her sister.

Trisha looked at it. She seemed to be contemplating for a few seconds before she wrinkled her tiny nose and shook her head.

"You're right," Sydney said and put it back. "Too glittery."

She walked deeper into the store, found a shirt and looked at it, but put it back immediately.

"There's nothing here," she said with a deep sigh. "We should try somewhere else."

"But we've been to almost every store," Trisha said.

"I know," Sydney said.

They walked out of the store.

"My feet are hurting," Trisha whined. "And I'm hungry."

"Let's go get something to eat then," Sydney said and grabbed her hand. They walked to the food court and got Chick-fil-A. They sat at a table and ate, Sydney worrying that they wouldn't find a present today and would have to come back another day. Sydney hated going to the mall. Too many people there. Too much noise and too many staring eyes.

A flock of girls from her school walked past, one of them whispering something to the others, making them laugh while staring at Sydney over their shoulders. Sydney ignored them.

"Santa," Trisha said.

Sydney froze. "Where?"

Trisha pointed at a poster telling them Santa would be on stage at the food court at two o'clock. Sydney looked at the stage and the long line, then at her watch. It was almost two.

"I wanna see Sa-a-nta," Trisha said.

Sydney started to pack up, throwing out the food they hadn't eaten and grabbed her backpack.

"No," she said.

"Please?" Trisha said.

Sydney shook her head and grabbed Trisha's hand in hers, then pulled her away, hurrying away from the food court.

"NO," she said, so harshly her sister almost started to cry.

45

We waited what felt like forever in that line. My feet were hurting and I was getting hungry. Tobias and Julie continued shopping on their own, every now and then texting me to let me know where they were. I just hoped I had given them enough money, but so far, they seemed to be doing fine.

The clock finally struck two o'clock and the lights turned on at the stage. A woman dressed as one of Santa's little helpers entered with a microphone in hand.

"Merry Christmas, children," she said, sounding hysterically merry. "Anyone here in the mood for a little Christmas song?"

I really wasn't.

"You better watch out," she started. *"Better not cry. Better not pout, I'm telling you why*...help me out here kids, why is it that we don't pout or cry? Can anyone tell me?"

She reached out the microphone to the kids, and they all squealed so loud it hurt my ears:

"SANTA CLAUS IS COMING TO TOWN!"

"That's right, kids," the lady said, then continued. *"He's making a list, he's checking it twice*...and why is that?"

Once again, the microphone was turned to the kids, who all, with no exception, screamed:

"HE'S GONNA FIND OUT WHO'S NAUGHTY OR NICE!"

"That's right, kids," the lady said, the bells on her elf hat jingling as she turned her head back and forth. "Now, let's sing the rest together. *He sees you when you're sleeping. He knows when you're awake, he knows if you've been bad or good, so be good for goodness sake."*

She stopped singing, then looked out at the kids and all their expectant eyes staring back at her, gleaming with anticipation.

"All right," she said and stepped aside. "Here's who you've all been waiting for, kids. H-E-E-R-E'S SANTA!"

Ferris wheel music followed before the curtain was pulled and Santa appeared, walking slowly, holding his belly, smiling behind the beard, waving with a loud:

"Ho-Ho-HO."

I knew he was just someone dressed up for the occasion, someone paid to do this job, but I still couldn't help but shiver slightly when seeing him. William, on the other hand, was ecstatic. He was waving and jumping up and down.

"Santa, Santa!"

Santa waved at the kids like he was some rock star, then sat on the big throne-like chair, laughing, his belly jumping up and down. The first kid in line was told he could go sit on Santa's lap and so he did.

"Now, have you been naughty or have you been nice this year, Mike?" Santa asked.

"Nice," Mike answered and Santa laughed again.

I calmed down, realizing there was nothing strange about this. Nothing out of the ordinary. It was just as it was supposed to be. I wondered if Sune was right, maybe I had let this entire craziness with Sydney and Sara Andrews get to me. I figured it was probably what Sara had said to me, the part about him coming for me now that she had told me her story. It was so ridiculous, I thought to myself. Silly, really. And it was about to ruin our nice Christmas. I wasn't going to let it. Maybe I had imagined the blood thing; maybe I had just gotten the kids all wound up thinking they saw what I saw. Maybe they didn't even see it, but only believed it because I had said so. There clearly wasn't anything in the chimney. And that tree in the living room and the things I saw in the ornaments. It was just my imagination running wild. It had to be. It was the only explanation. Maybe we all had gotten a little carried away and just thought we saw it. Maybe it had all just gotten a little out of hand.

"Who's next?" Santa said and I realized it was William's turn.

"Off you go," I said and pushed him slightly toward the stage. "Go give Santa that binky."

I walked behind him, keeping close to him as he

approached Santa, arms stretched out so the man could pick him up and put him in his lap.

"Ho. Ho. Ho. And who do we have here?"

"William," Will said.

I signaled for him to take out the binky, then nodded when he did as he was told.

"Well, hello there, William," Santa said, his voice deep and jolly.

William was holding the binky in his hand.

"Give it to him," I mouthed.

"Oh, you want me to have that?" Santa asked.

William looked like he was considering it for a few seconds, then nodded eagerly. I smiled and took his photo with my phone to remind him when he started asking about his binky. The deal was that Santa would bring him a big present for Christmas in exchange for the pacifier. It had worked for other parents and I hoped it would for us too. Now, all I needed to know was what the boy wanted for it.

"Have you been a good boy, William?" Santa asked putting the binky in the pocket of his red suit. "Or have you been NAUGHTY?"

"Good boy," William squealed. "Good boy."

"And what does such a good boy want for Christmas?" Santa asked.

This was the moment when I was supposed to listen very carefully to make sure he got whatever he told Santa, but I had stopped listening. I was staring at the photo on my screen, mouth agape. In the photo, Santa's eyes were glowing red like Christmas globes, his fingers had long dirty nails, and his teeth, don't even let me get started on his teeth.

"What do you want for Christmas, little boy?" Santa repeated when Will didn't answer.

I was staring at the Santa sitting with my son on his lap, looking perfectly normal. But down on my screen, the picture was completely different.

"Okay, my good boy," Santa said and put him down. "Maybe you'll tell me next time we meet."

I grabbed William's hand in mine and pulled him away, still staring at Santa, my hands shaking as we walked away.

"Was that the real Santa, Mommy?" William asked. "Was it?"

I shook my head and cleared my throat. "Of course not, William. Of course, it wasn't. Santa is way too busy to sit here in some mall. He has to get all the presents done by Christmas, remember?"

"Right." William turned his head and looked back at the man in the red suit as I rushed him away from the food court.

"But who was he, then, Mommy? Who was that man?"

I felt a chill run down my spine as I finally spotted Tobias and Julie and waved at them, rushing to them so we could get out of this place in a hurry.

"I don't know, sweetie," I said. "I really don't know."

46

It was getting ridiculous. They had been in every store in the entire mall, many of them twice. They had eaten lunch and dinner there and still hadn't found a present for their mother.

Sydney was upset. What if they never found one? They could hardly have Christmas without a present for their mother. Trisha was getting tired and whiny as Sydney dragged her around the mall, going into store after store, looking at everything on the shelves.

"Why don't we just give her that apron I found in Macy's? You liked that," she said, tired.

"No," Sydney said and dragged her sister inside Books-A-Million.

"Why not? It was fun. It said MAY THE FORKS BE WITH YOU," Trisha said. "It's like *Star Wars* and Mommy loves *Star Wars*."

"Would you like to get a present that said, *hey, woman, get back in the kitchen where you belong?* No. I want this to be a present Mom will be excited about, one that will cheer her up, not one that tells her that we only see her as someone who'll cook for us and serve us."

"But she's not," Trisha said. "Not anymore. You're always cooking for us. She never cooks anymore."

"Exactly," Sydney said. "I don't to make her feel bad by giving her an apron. Just like I didn't want to give her a new pan or those utensils you wanted to give her. It has to be something spectacular. It has to be."

"Why?"

"Because it has to be. It simply HAS to be!"

Sydney was yelling now. She felt how her nostrils were flaring and could tell she was scaring her sister. She calmed down.

"I'm sorry," she said and ran a hand through her hair. "I'm just so tired and I want to find the right thing."

They left the bookstore. Sydney looked around at the many stores surrounding them, not knowing which one to go into next.

"How about a scented candle?" Trisha asked.

"No. You already suggested that once," Sydney said.

"Some underwear from Victoria's Secret?"

"No!"

Sydney felt the mall spinning around her. So many voices, faces, and bodies swarming around her. Some were laughing, some were fighting, others just looking, not uttering a word to one another, lots were on their phones until they bumped into someone.

"Where are we going now?" her sister asked.

"I don't know," Sydney answered.

And then she saw it. The small shop that was squeezed in between Islander Comic & Collectibles and Vitamin World. In the window, they had a dog, a rescue puppy. Its big brown eyes looked back at her.

"I know exactly what we should give her," she said and approached the window.

"A puppy?" Trisha squealed with happiness. She could hardly breathe. "That's a good idea."

Sydney smiled. The puppy could keep her mother company when she felt lonely, especially when they were both in school and even at night when she felt lonely in bed, it could sleep with her. It would get her out of the house too, to go on walks. Sydney had read online it was very important for people in grief to get outside and get some fresh air and that having a dog was a good way to move on.

"It is a great idea," Sydney said and looked at it through the glass. "It's the perfect gift."

47

Sune was in the kitchen when we got home. Much to my surprise, he smiled when we walked in. The smile seemed a little manic, but at this point, I would take any type when coming from him.

"I baked," he said.

I stared at him, then at the kids, who stood with their jaws dropped, eyes wide gazing at him.

"You what?" I asked.

Sune rolled to the oven, grabbed some oven mitts, and pulled out what appeared to be a cake.

"Chocolate cake," he said.

The kids and I exchanged glances. Theirs said: *What's going on?*

I shrugged for an answer, then mouthed: *I don't know.*

Sune held the cake out between his hands. It smelled really good but slightly burnt.

"What are you all looking at me like that for? I thought you'd be hungry when you got back."

"It's just...you've never baked before, Sune," I said.

"I know," he said. "There's a first time for everything, right? I figured I might as well make the best of my time. I'm sick of just sitting here, doing nothing. It is, after all, Christmas, right?"

He rolled back to the oven and burned his finger when closing it. I looked at the kids again. They seemed more scared than happy. I was thrilled to see Sune in a good mood and finally out of the media room. I was terrified of ruining it, of hurting him somehow.

"That's great, Sune," I said and gestured for them to say something encouraging as well. "Right kids?"

"Yes, Dad," Tobias said. "It's really great."

"It smells weird," Julie said.

"Julie!"

"What?" she said. "I can't be honest now?"

Sune looked disappointedly at the cake. "I think it cooked too long."

"That's okay," I said, feeling awful. Here he was, trying for once to actually do something. He had been so depressed for so long. I really wanted him to feel good about himself. "I love burnt cake."

"I love chocolate cake," William exclaimed. He found a stool and climbed up so he could sit by the counter.

Sune smiled, then cut him a piece. William dug in and, if he was pretending to enjoy it, he was a very good actor. But that was William for you. He would eat anything. I urged the big kids to sit down as well and grabbed a knife to help Sune cut the cake for them.

"Don't," he said as I approached him.

"I'm sorry?"

"You don't have to help me. I can do it. I am perfectly capable of cutting the cake myself."

"I didn't mean to...I was..."

"Just trying to help. Yes, I know. But you do this all the time. You take over like I'm some kid who needs help. I need to do things on my own. I'm sick of being unable to do stuff."

I backed up, wondering what had suddenly gotten into him. "Okay."

He cut the cake and handed the kids each a piece. He accidentally pushed one plate over the edge of the countertop and it shattered all over the floor. Sune growled, annoyed. I jumped up to help, but he stopped me.

"It's okay. I've got this. I don't need to be saved, Rebekka. I can do this. I don't need you to take care of me constantly."

I sat back down while Sune reached forward to grab the broken pieces from the floor. We all stared at him struggling to reach, but no one dared to help. Sune growled and picked a big piece up, then reached down for yet another one and cut his finger so it bled. Sune grumbled and looked at the bleeding finger. Tobias looked at me for help. I took in a deep breath, then said:

"You need me to get a Band-Aid?"

Sune, still staring at the finger, shook his head. "That's

okay." He rolled across the tiles and through the living room.

"I think I'll just...take a nap."

As he disappeared once again into the media room, I sighed and looked at the kids, my heart breaking. Tobias had tears in his eyes that he tried bravely to hold back.

"How about we watch a movie, huh, kids?"

William squealed with excitement, *"Beauty and the Beast!"*

"Oh, no!" Julie said.

Tobias added, "Not again."

48

We settled on the *Emoji Movie*. Julie was on her phone for most of the time, while Tobias and William seemed to be the only two actually watching it since I couldn't concentrate. I kept looking at the door to the media room, secretly wishing it would open and Sune would come back out and be with us. He loved watching movies.

Finally, I decided to go in instead. I knocked, then opened the door carefully and peeked inside.

"Sune?"

"Go away, Rebekka," he said.

I walked in anyway. I sat down on the couch that he was using as a bed. It seemed like it hadn't been used at all since I put the sheets on it.

"Have you been sleeping in your chair?"

"Who cares, Rebekka?"

I shook my head, feeling awful, realizing that all this

time he had needed my help. I hadn't even thought about the fact that he had a hard time getting out of the chair on his own. He had learned how to go to the bathroom on his own, but the couch was way too low for him to be able to get there on his own.

"You have, haven't you? You haven't been able to get yourself onto the couch on your own. Why didn't you ask me to help you?" I asked.

"Because we were fighting, remember?"

"So, now you're suddenly too proud to ask for help?" I asked.

"Well...I wanted to be able to do stuff on my own. Now that I finally have realized that I'll never walk again."

I had never heard him say those words before. After the accident, he kept telling me he would walk again, and it didn't matter how many doctors told him he wouldn't, he kept telling me would, that one day he would.

"What's with you these days?" I asked and reached out my hand toward him. I think I already knew what was going on. He had put all his hope in this doctor over here, in the Promised Land and when he finally told him that he couldn't help him, he lost hope.

"It's true, Rebekka," he said, still not looking at me. "I'm never going to walk again. I know the doctors have told me repeatedly, but I refused to listen. Guess the joke is on me, right?"

"What? No, no. Sune, you're getting it all wrong. That's not what Dr. Herman told you at all."

"Yes, it was, Rebekka. He said it was all in my head. Do you have any idea how that made me feel? Before that, I always thought it was all physical. Yet, I believed I could somehow fix it or train it away with the right trainer or right program or even the right medicine. Now that he told me it was in my head, how can I ever beat that, huh? There's no cure, no pill, and no surgery I can have done to make this better. I am doing this to myself. It's all me. I can't fight myself. I can't get rid of myself. How, Rebekka? How am I supposed to do this?"

I understood what he was saying, and I even got why he would feel that way, but I wasn't ready to give up just yet.

"I don't know, Sune, but I still believe you will. If you don't give up. You can't give up on yourself. I won't let you."

"Well, I have," he said and looked me in the eyes.

What I saw in them was devastating. I realized he had finally completely lost all hope. "This is who I am now," he said and looked down at himself. "It's not going to pass, Rebekka. It's not going away. And I am not going to destroy your life as well. That's why I have to let you go. It's not fair to ask you to stay with me. You're free to go and live your life as you please. I won't hold you back. Now, please, leave. I want to be alone."

"But Sune..."

"Leave, please."

I got up, but I didn't want to leave. I wanted to wrap my arms around him, I wanted to kiss him and tell him everything was going to be all right, that we would get through this, together.

"LEAVE!"

I walked out, closed the door behind me, then slid my back down against it, crying.

49

"I can't sell you a puppy."

Sydney glared at the woman behind the counter.

"Why not? I have the money right here." Sydney held the fifty-dollar bill up for the lady to see.

She shook her head. "First of all, we're an adoption center, so we don't sell puppies; people adopt them from us. But I can't do it. Not without your parent's consent."

"But...But...It's *for* our parent, for our mother," Sydney said. "We want to give it to her for Christmas."

"To make her feel better," Trisha added. "She's been so sad since our dad died. We think a puppy will make her happy."

The lady sighed. "Look. I can tell that you really want this and it's a nice thought, it really is, and maybe you can bring her here and then she can take the puppy home, but I can't sell it to you. Not without an adult." She tilted her head and smiled. "I'm sorry."

Sydney and Trisha left the store, shoulders slumped.

The puppy in the window stared disappointedly at them and followed them with its brown eyes as they disappeared down toward the shops they had already been in several times. Time was running out and soon there was an announcement over the speakers that the mall was about to close.

"We've got to hurry up," Sydney said. She pulled her sister's arm as they ran into a store, then out of it because they couldn't find anything there either, then back into another store but nothing was good enough there either.

"How about the apron?" Trisha said.

Sydney sighed. It was beginning to sound like a good idea, the apron, even though she felt bad for giving her mother such a lousy gift. It had to be better than nothing, right?

It's the thought that counts. That's what they all say, right?

"Okay," she said. "Let's go get that stupid apron."

She held her sister's hand as they walked toward Macy's when Trisha suddenly stopped in front of a store window.

"Look, Syd," she said and pointed.

Sydney looked at the storefront. She had never seen it before. They hadn't been inside this one. That was strange. She thought they had been in all of the stores in the entire mall.

"Look," Trisha said again.

Sydney looked at what she was pointing at. A small necklace glistened in the light from above. It consisted of three parts, put together they shaped a heart. On the part to the left, it said *little sister,* on the one to the right, it said *big sister*, and on the one in the middle it said *mommy*. It was gorgeous. So sparkling and so...so...perfect.

Sydney's face lit up. This was even better than the puppy and less demanding. This way, their mother would always remember her children and how much she loved them and that they were there for her through everything in life. Sydney and Trisha looked at each other and smiled.

"Let's go get it," Trisha said and opened the door to the store. "If we hurry, I think we can make it before the mall closes."

50

Sydney looked at the necklace inside the store.

"It's perfect," Trisha said.

"I know," Sydney said.

It cost fifty dollars. Exactly the amount Sydney had in her hand. She turned to look for someone to help her buy it but couldn't see anyone. Sydney walked to the counter but there was no one there.

"Hello?" she said. "We'd like to buy a necklace. Hello?"

"There's no one here," Trisha said.

"Of course, there's someone here. There has to be. Otherwise, people could just take the stuff and leave."

"Maybe they went home?" Trisha said. She looked back into the mall where people were rushing by the window to get home. "The mall is about to close."

"I know," Sydney said, drumming her fingers impatiently on the counter. "They're probably just cleaning up in the back or something. You know, getting ready to leave. They probably didn't hear us come in." She leaned over the counter. "Hello?"

Still, no one came. Sydney was getting annoyed. She had been looking all day for the perfect gift and now she had finally found it. All she needed was to buy it, then she could go home and have a wonderful Christmas with her mother and sister. She was so close.

"Hello?"

Sydney walked past the counter and looked into the back. But she couldn't see anyone there. On the speakers, they were telling people it was the last chance to get out of the mall before it closed. A woman rushed past the window carrying multiple bags in her hands.

Trisha tugged her sister's shirt. "We should go."

Sydney sighed, annoyed. "We're so close."

"We have to come back tomorrow then," Trisha said.

Sydney really didn't want to have to come back again. She was right there; the necklace was right over there. All she needed was for someone to help her get it and then pay.

"Hell-o-o-o! Is someone there?" she asked again.

"They're not here," Trisha said and tugged harder on her shirt. "They went home and so should we."

But wouldn't they have locked the shop up before leaving? Sydney asked herself. She shrugged with a sigh.

"All right then. We'll come back tomorrow."

They walked toward the exit when the shutters suddenly rolled down with a loud thud, blocking all the windows and the door. Trisha shrieked, grabbing her sister's hand in hers, squeezing it tightly.

Next, the lights went out.

"Syd!"

Sydney's heart was pounding in her chest, but she forced herself to stay calm. For her sister's sake.

"It's okay," she said. "It's just because they're closing."

"But they closed the shutters," her sister said, her voice trembling. "And they shut off the lights."

"I know," Sydney said, trying to think fast, trying to figure out what to do. She had a cellphone so they could always call for their mother, but she really wanted to avoid that. Her mother had enough trouble as it was. "We just need to find...there must be a way out in the back or something."

Holding on tightly to her sister's hand, she turned around and walked toward the back when she heard the sound of jingle bells cutting through the darkness.

51

Sydney's heart stopped. She grabbed Trisha and pulled her close. The sound of jingling bells crept closer.

"What is that?" Trisha asked. "That sound?"

"I don't know," Sydney said. "Stay close to me."

"I'm scared," Trisha said.

"Me too," Sydney said.

"What if we can't get out of here?"

Sydney held her breath as the tinkling sound grew closer still. She recognized the sound as the very same one she had heard at night. Until now, she had believed she was going nuts, that it was all in her head, something she had made up because of the death of her father. But now she knew it wasn't. This was real. He was real and he was here.

Trisha screamed. "What's that?"

Sydney looked in front of them and spotted the red glowing globes. She took a step backward as the sound of laughter filled the store, the deep well-known laugh that, for most people, meant joy and happiness, but filled Sydney with the deepest sense of terror.

"It's Santa," Trisha exclaimed, happily. "Santa can help us get out, can't he? He can get us out of here. Santa likes children. He'll help us, don't you think so, Sydney? Syd?"

Sydney walked backward, pulling her sister with her as the glowing red globes approached them. She had a feeling this particular Santa wasn't there to help them. There was something in the way he laughed, in the sound of the bells that made the hairs stand up on her neck. She thought about that lady, Sara Andrews, and what she had said in court when she told her side of the story, the one that everyone assumed was just a crazy woman trying to get out of being killed for what she had done.

We let this guy into our homes every year without realizing who he really is, what he really is.

Everyone had laughed at her. The media mocked her. Only Sydney had listened carefully. Because she had read what her dad had written on that notepad right before he died. And she knew. She knew his death wasn't natural. She knew something else was at stake and she wondered why no one else ever stopped to think: What if this lady is right? What if she's onto something? And then she pondered if that was what it felt like to be insane.

Santa is just an anagram for Satan.

"I think we need to get out of here," she whispered to her sister. "Come. Follow me."

They turned around and ran for the door. Sydney grabbed the handle and pulled it, but of course, it was locked. They clenched their fists and hammered on the shuttered windows, screaming and yelling for help, but there was no one out there. The mall was empty and all they could hear was the sound of jingle bells, as it came closer and closer still.

Slowly, Sydney turned around and looked straight into the red glowing eyes. She didn't see it happen but felt the pain as his teeth sunk in, as they penetrated the skin on her neck. After that, there was nothing more. Only darkness and the sound of a deep rumbling laughter. As Sydney sunk into oblivion, all she could think about was her poor mother and how lonely she was going to be with her gone too.

52

I spent the evening on the couch in the living room while the kids watched *Beauty and the Beast*—again. Julie went to her room to be on her computer. But Tobias stayed with William and me, keeping us company. I was on my iPad, but my mind was elsewhere.

"You think my dad will come with us to Disney World when we go?" Tobias suddenly asked.

I looked up. His eyes met mine. I saw such sadness in them, it was almost unbearable. He was suffering in this whole affair with his father. Sune had no time for him, no energy to spend with him, and I could only imagine what it was doing to him to watch his father lose hope like this. It had to be tough. I was the only one he really talked to, but even I hadn't had much time for him in the past couple of years.

"I'm sure he will," I said.

We both knew I was lying. I wasn't so sure about anything concerning Sune right now. I was devastated to have seen him lose hope and I had no idea how to help him get it back. Especially since he had made it clear that he didn't want my help anymore. He wanted to get by on his own, to show the world he could take care of himself.

And he wanted me out of his life.

I looked back at the screen when something popped up. I was reading the local newspaper *Florida Today* when a story broke. BREAKING NEWS, it said, but that wasn't what caught my attention. It was the words that followed. SANTA-SHOOTER FOUND DEAD.

I pressed the link and the story opened up. I held my breath as I read about Sara Andrews and how she was found dead in her prison cell on the morning after I visited her, hung from the ceiling with a string of Christmas lights wrapped around her neck. Where she got the lights, the prison couldn't say.

The article then continued on about who she was and how she had been convicted of killing her ex-husband on Christmas Eve and how she believed Santa was out to get her and had made her life miserable.

I read it all with a pounding heart, then put the iPad down, found my phone, and walked outside. I found Sydney Hahn's number and dialed it. It was warm out and the cicadas were singing. Christmas decorations had been hung on the lampposts, wishing us all a Merry Christmas. I was beginning to wonder just how merry it was going to be.

"Pick up. Pick up," I said when the phone continued to ring. "Come on, Sydney."

The voicemail message came on and I hung up, then

pressed redial and waited again. I couldn't stop thinking about Sara Andrews and her story and even more about her words.

He'll come after you too.

I had to talk to Sydney and let her know. I wanted to warn her, to tell her to be careful, but she still didn't pick up. I tried again.

This time, it was picked up. I sighed with relief.

"Sydney? It's Rebekka..."

There was heavy breathing at the other end. It didn't sound like it would come from her.

"Sydney?"

"Rebekka?" A voice said. It wasn't Sydney's. This belonged to a man, a man with a very deep voice.

"Who's this?" I asked, heart pounding in my chest. "Who is this? What have you done to Sydney? What have you DONE?"

"Tell me, Rebekka," the voice said. "Have you been nice this year or have you been a NAUGHTY GIRL?"

"S-Santa?"

PART IV

53

I wasn't even enjoying the coffee. I was sitting on a soft couch at Café Juice 'N Java while staring anxiously at the front door.

He was running late. At least by five minutes.

I sighed and sipped the coffee, my heart worried. I was the one who had called him. Right after I had hung up on Santa, I called detective Ryder and asked him to find Sydney Hahn since I feared something bad had happened to her. I couldn't explain how I knew. I mean, how could I? What was I supposed to say?

I also told him to look for the red marks on Sara's body. He complained that he was busy and didn't have time for this, but I told him it was important. He simply had to do it.

Now, two days had passed and he had finally called me back. I was sick with worry. He told me to meet him here at the café. My fingers were drumming on the armrest as I spotted him. He held the door for some lady, then entered. He didn't smile when he saw me.

He ordered a coffee, then sat down across from me. He threw a file on the table.

"You were right," he said.

"Right about what?"

"The red marks. They were on her neck just as you told me they would be. The autopsy report concluded they were bug bites. Now, my question to you is, how did you know about the marks? How could you possibly know when the woman was in a prison cell?"

I sighed. "Oh, boy."

He leaned forward. "It's all a little crazy, don't you think? Something very strange is going on and I can't seem to find any ups or downs to this. That was why I asked you to meet me here instead of at the office. I can't make anything out of this, no silver lining. I can't risk any of my colleagues hearing about this crazy stuff. But now I need you to tell me, what the heck is going on?"

I rubbed my hands together. I was nervous. "First, I need you to tell me if you found Sydney Hahn. I haven't eaten anything or closed an eye in two nights worrying about her."

He looked surprised. "You haven't heard?"

My heart sunk. I shook my head, fearing what would come next. "No. No, I haven't."

"Oh, dear Lord," he said. "That night you called me and told me to look for her, I went to her mother's house and she told me Sydney and her sister had gone to the mall and been gone all day. We found them inside one of the smaller shops..."

"What do you mean you found them?"

"Sydney. She was...dead. Her chest was ripped open. Her sister was sitting in a corner of the shop, hiding behind the shelves, crying helplessly. She kept screaming when we asked her questions, and what she said made no sense, none at all."

I swallowed. I felt awful, broken. "What did she say?"

"She kept screaming about Santa. It was all she kept saying. *Santa, evil. Santa, evil.* We couldn't get anything else out of her."

"And where is she now?"

"She's still in the hospital. She wasn't hurt but no one knows what to do about her. Her mother can't even calm her down. I hear they're talking about putting her away in an institution on the mainland. It's the shock, the doctors say. The trauma. But we believe she must have seen the killer and that he was probably wearing a Santa outfit."

I sighed and leaned back, a million through rushing through my mind. "I don't think he's an ordinary killer," I said. "I'm not even sure he's human."

Jack Ryder wrinkled his forehead. "What do you mean?"

"Sit tight," I said and reached into my backpack. I pulled out all the copies I had made lately during my research and showed it to him.

"What's all this?"

"Your killer," I said.

54

We went through it all together. Every page, every article I had found and, for hours, I spoke about everything Sydney had told me, what Sara Andrews had said, and then about my own experiences.

"Really?" he said, skeptically. "Blood? In the chimney?"

"I swear to you, it was there. I saw it again last night when I couldn't sleep and walked across the living room. It was there. It was the sound that made me stop at first. The dripping sound. Then I turned on a light and saw it. Blood running down the chimney. I swear, I also heard a scraping sound coming from the inside of the chimney. Like long nails scraping on the sides of it. I keep imagining these soot-caked claws scraping inside the brick belly of the chimney. I am not making this up, Detective. And the pictures I took at the mall. I looked through my phone yesterday. All gone. Simply vanished."

"So, you have no proof of anything you're saying?"

Jack Ryder said. I could tell he was trying to understand, trying to believe me, but found it harder and harder.

"I'm afraid not. But I have been doing a lot of research," I said and showed him the many articles. "These are all victims of this. All killed in the month of December since the city of Cocoa Beach was established in nineteen twenty-five. Back then, they knew something was up; they even wrote about it in the local paper, how some people claimed to have heard jingle bells at night and strange sounds coming from inside their chimneys. The story back then went that there was a young boy in nineteen-twenty-seven, who—while playing hide and go seek with his friend—climbed into the chimney of his house and got stuck. The friend went home and later that same night his dad then lit a fire and killed the boy. The first victim that was found dead in a chimney was in December nineteen twenty-eight. It was believed back then that it was him, the boy from the year before that had later returned to haunt the city and kill people as revenge for what happened back then. In the modern day, the story was lost and later just called old superstition, a spooky story to tell your kids so they wouldn't crawl up into the chimney. But what if it is real, Detective, huh? What if this story is real?"

Jack Ryder looked at me with a deep sigh. "And you say that they all have the same red marks?"

"All of them that I have been able to get my hands on. Sydney was the one who showed me."

"I'm not sure I even want to know how she found out," he said. "But let me get this straight. You're telling me you believe this killer is...some type of a ghost? Or what?"

I shrugged. "An entity of sorts. I don't know. Something evil, haunting this town. Does it have to have a name? Not everything in life comes with a box you can fit it in."

Jack Ryder sighed and rubbed his stubble. He was very tanned for someone who worked a lot. I knew he surfed, so I guessed that was why. Apparently, everyone in this town surfed. Even the mayor could be found in the waves if they were good. I was even told that, if the waves were really good, all the shops and restaurants downtown would be closed and there would be small signs in the windows saying: GONE SURFING.

Jack Ryder was still thinking, looking through the papers on the table. I sipped my coffee, then he said:

"I have to admit that when looking at Sydney's chest, I knew something was really wrong. There was no way a human could have done that. Had we found her outside somewhere, I would have believed it was a panther or maybe a bear, but this was inside the mall. Inside. Everything was closed, all the windows and doors were locked, even the shutters were closed. No animal could have gotten in and out."

"How about security cameras? Did they have them at the store?" I asked.

Jack Ryder looked up and nodded. "That's the oddest part. There was nothing on them. Nothing but static. It looked like freaking snow." He paused, then continued:

"That's not completely true, there was something on them. A sound. The sound of jingle bells."

I leaned back on the couch. "You said it yourself, Detective. Something strange is going on here. Something really strange. And, to be honest, it's beginning to freak me out."

Jack Ryder nodded. "You and me both. You and me both."

55

Alyssa had a hard time concentrating at school. Night after night, she was awoken by the sounds coming from downstairs, but she had stopped going down there. Not since she had seen her brother. She didn't dare to. Yet, the sounds were still there every night and it scared her like crazy. But with the lack of sleep and with everything that was going on, her grades had started to slide. She had gotten an F on her math test for the second week in a row.

It had her parents worried.

"I know things are tough right now," her mother told her when she had the talk with her in the kitchen after she had come home from school and she saw the test in her backpack. "But we have got to keep living. We can't just let everything slide. You've got to focus on school."

Alyssa stared at her mother, looked into her eyes. She wanted so badly to tell her that the only reason she had done badly on another test was that she couldn't concentrate because she was so tired, so exhausted from lack of sleep. It was like the words on the test paper danced and made no sense. She wanted to tell her mother about what she had seen that night. That she had seen her brother, who wasn't her brother anymore, and that *thing*. That awful thing, a beast with long pointy teeth that had grabbed for her and how terrified she had been that he would run up the stairs after her, or that he would come to her room at night. He was down there at night, she just knew he was, and every night she sat under the covers shaking, listening to every sound in the house, praying that he wouldn't find his way to her door. Oftentimes, she would find herself staring at the door handle for hours, terrified that it would turn. She wanted to tell her mother about the sound of jingling bells that kept her awake. She wanted to tell her how scared she was all night long. And not just at night anymore. She often heard strange noises during the day as well. But she knew her mother wouldn't understand. She would tell her it was only in her mind. Alyssa feared they would think she was crazy and put her away in some mental institution, where they would shock her or medicate her till she never spoke of crazy stuff like this again.

"I'll get better," she said. "I promise."

Her mother smiled. It wasn't a very happy smile. "That's good, sweetie. It will soon be Christmas break and hopefully, things will get better after that. We could all use a little break, huh?"

Christmas. Christmas Eve night, that's when he comes, isn't it? That's when he is planning on killing me, isn't it?

"Honey. You're shivering. Are you all right?"

"I'm fine," she said. The last thing she wanted was for her mother to think she was sick and have her stay home from school. She needed to get away from the house, away from the chimney.

"I'm perfectly fine," she repeated, just to make sure her mother had heard her.

Her mother smiled again, a little more genuine this time, then got up and walked to the stove. "Good. I thought I would try and cook a little tonight. Would be good for a change, huh? I'm getting tired of all that pizza."

She turned to look at Alyssa for some sort of confirmation that she agreed, but Alyssa wasn't listening anymore. She had gotten up from her chair in the kitchen and stood where the kitchen became the living room and stared at the chimney. She was hearing loud scraping sounds coming from the chimney.

"Alyssa?" her mom said and approached her. "Are you all right? You're acting a little weird."

She looked up at her mother, her body shaking. "It's that sound."

"What sound, sweetie?"

The sound was loud in her ears, sounding like an animal trying to dig its way out of the brick chimney.

"You don't hear it?"

Her mother listened, then shook her head. She felt Alyssa's forehead. "Are you sure you're feeling all right?"

"I'm fine," Alyssa said, trying to sound convincing, but she could hear how her voice was shaking.

The doorbell rang and Alyssa's mom went to open it.

Meanwhile, Alyssa kept staring at the chimney, wondering when that thing—whatever it was—that was trying to dig its way out of it would succeed.

56

"Rebekka Franck? What a surprise."

I smiled at Jackie. Her pale face smiled back. She had lost a lot of weight since I saw her last.

"To what do we owe the honor?"

"I'm actually here to see Alyssa if that's okay with you?"

Jackie looked perplexed at me, then nodded. "Sure. Come on in. She just got back from school."

I walked into the living room and spotted Alyssa at the other end. She looked frightened and, as I stepped closer, I immediately knew why.

I turned to look at the chimney as I heard the scraping sound that I recognized from my own house.

"What a nice surprise," her mother said behind me while closing the door.

I gasped and looked at Alyssa. Our eyes met and we both knew.

"Alyssa? Rebekka is here. She wants to talk to you. Can I get you anything?" she asked, addressed to me.

"If you have some coffee, that would be great," I said, mostly to get her out of the room.

I approached Alyssa, our eyes still locked, while the scraping sounds filled our ears.

"You hear it too?" I asked in a whisper.

She bit her lip. I could tell she was afraid to say it. I knew how she felt. I sometimes felt like I was going crazy when hearing and seeing these things, and talking about it just made it worse. I had tried to talk to Sune about it, but he wouldn't listen. He thought I was losing it. I was beginning to think I was too. The only thing that kept me going was the fact that I knew the kids had seen the blood too. And now the look in Alyssa's eyes told me I wasn't alone.

"You hear it too?" Alyssa whispered.

I nodded. "At my house. Sometimes it's bells, sometimes it's scraping sounds like these, and sometimes it's like a pulse or a drumming sound."

"It's like someone is in there, trying to get out," she said.

I nodded. We both looked at the chimney, hearts pounding in our chests. "So, I'm not going insane?" she asked.

I shook my head. "That's actually why I came. You know Sydney Hahn? Or maybe I should call her SH14?"

Alyssa nodded. "Sure. From my chat room. She lost her dad."

"She was killed."

Alyssa's eyes grew wide. She made a sound that I could only interpret as surprise or maybe fear.

"I think it was the same killer who killed your brother," I said, still keeping my voice low. Jackie was still in the kitchen. It sounded like she was looking for something in the cabinets; she was also mumbling something about cookies. I had to be fast now before she returned.

"What...what was it?"

"We don't know. But I came here because you wrote something in the chat, something about you seeing your dead brother in the living room. I went to Sydney's house and talked to her mother. She let me go through her computer and that's how I found out. You really should get a better profile name. If I could find you that easily, then anyone could," I said.

Alyssa sighed. "H-h-he was right here," she said and pointed. He was looking at me and asking me what my favorite holiday was. His was Christmas, he said."

"I take it he looked like your brother?" I asked.

She nodded. "But it wasn't him. I knew it wasn't. And then he ch-changed."

"Changed?"

Alyssa's eyes were on me. She nodded. "He became something else. Something I can't even describe. It started with the teeth...long pointy teeth grew out of his face, and then there were the eyes."

"What about the eyes?"

"They were red."

I swallowed hard. "Red? Like two..."

"Red glowing Christmas globes," we both said in unison.

Alyssa's mother came in from the kitchen holding a tray between her hands, smiling from ear to ear. "Cookies," she said. "I found cookies. They might be a little old, but I hope they'll do."

57

We ate the cookies. They were stale and dry, but out of politeness, we ate them, still hearing the scraping sounds and pretending not to, while I sipped the coffee, smiling at Jackie.

I told her I was there to talk to Alyssa about arranging something for Sydney's funeral since her mother was too out of it to do anything herself. Jackie didn't seem to know who Sydney was so we told her it was a girl from school that we both knew, and she seemed to accept that. I told her I got to know Sydney while vacationing here, and luckily, she didn't ask for details. We drank our coffee and ate the cookies for about an hour when I told them I had to leave.

Alyssa walked me to the front door, then leaned over and whispered. "I'm scared."

I looked at her, then stroked her cheek gently. "Me too," I said. "Lock the door to your room at night and, whatever you do, don't go near the chimney. Promise me that? I gave you my number. So, call me if you need me, okay? If anything happens, just call."

She nodded and I left, feeling like I was leaving her in the lion's den. It felt so good to get out of the house and away from the scraping sound. It seemed to be a lot worse at her house than mine and, as I entered our own beach house further down the road, I was delighted to hear nothing but the sound of Tobias and Julie fighting over something. I hadn't told them where I went, just that I was going for a run. I yelled that I was back, then jumped in the shower. When I came out, William was standing in my bedroom with tear-filled eyes.

"Now what?" I asked.

"Ju-Ju!" he said and pointed.

"Was she teasing you again?"

He nodded with a sniffle. "I miss my binky," he said, wiping his nose on his sleeve. "She called me a baby."

I smiled and took Will in my arms. "You're not a baby," I said. "You're a big boy now. A big boy who doesn't need his binky anymore."

He sniffled again, then nodded. "Big boy."

"There you go."

"Mo-om?" It was Julie. She came into the bedroom too, Tobias right behind her.

"It's a party now," I said smiling.

"When are we going to Disney World?"

I sighed. It was a question the kids asked every day now. I had promised I'd take them, but I was worried about Sune. Would he come? I had told him it was probably not a problem to navigate a wheelchair around

Disney World, but he didn't seem very thrilled about the idea of spending the entire day there, having all those staring eyes at him and kids pointing fingers and asking their parents *What is wrong with that man?* Or even worse, hearing the parents tell them *Not to stare.*

I had kept postponing it, but time was running out. Christmas was coming up in a week and it had to be before then. Plus, I was eager to get out of this strange house and maybe even the entire town. It was starting to get on my nerves.

"You know what? Let me talk to your dad about doing it tomorrow, okay?"

58

"I'm not going."

"You can't be serious."

I was looking at Sune. As usual, he was sitting in the media room, looking out the window, his back turned to me.

"Well, I am. I'm not going to Disney World."

"Sune," I said. "Your kids have been looking forward to going ever since we told them about this trip. They want you to be there. They want to experience it all with their dad. Don't you get that? You're missing out on everything. This trip could have been so much fun if you took part in some of the stuff we do. Going to Kennedy Space Center would have been a lot more fun if you had been with us. The kids asked about you all the time. Tobias was so worried, he could hardly enjoy it. You can't seriously tell me you don't want to go to Disney World?"

He shrugged. "Well, I'm very sorry that the fact that I can't walk has destroyed your vacation time."

"That's not what I meant and you know it perfectly well. You're twisting my words again."

He sighed. "It's not like I'm missing out on anything. I can't go on any rides anyway."

I stomped my feet in anger. "Damn it, Sune! We're not going to Disney for your sake. We're going for the kids. Go for them, not yourself. For once, get your head out of your bellybutton, will you?"

I growled, turned around and left, slamming the door behind me. I was so sick of this, so tired of him feeling sorry for himself.

But as soon as I had slammed the door, I was overwhelmed with guilt. Who was I to get angry with him? I knew nothing about what it was like to be in his position.

"I take it he's not coming?" Tobias said.

"Are we not going to Disney tomorrow, then?" Julie asked concerned.

William looked up from the drawing he was making on the breakfast counter, a whimper emerging from his lips.

"Oh, we're going," I said as I opened the fridge and pulled out some dough to make a fresh batch of cookies. I was determined to make this the best Christmas ever, no matter whether Sune participated or not.

"And we're going to have a great time."

The kids looked at one another. Only William cheered. The two others smiled but didn't dare say anything out loud.

The next day, when we were all getting ready to go,

the door to the media room suddenly opened and Sune pushed his chair out.

I stared at him, mouth agape. "You dressed?" I looked at his wet hair. "And showered?"

He smiled. "I can hardly go to Disney World wearing the same thing I've worn for the past week, now can I? I mean, I might meet Mickey and you can't be dirty when meeting Mickey, can you?"

The kids could hardly contain their excitement, and frankly, neither could I. "Let's go then," I said and shooed the kids into the car, then helped Sune get in as well.

"I might have made a mess on the bathroom floor," he said in a low voice. "It's a little flooded."

I smiled, then leaned over and kissed him. It took both of us by surprise. We hadn't been close in a very long time. "I'm sure it's okay," I said. "I'm sure it will be just fine."

59

Disney World's Magic Kingdom was even more overwhelming than I had imagined. And so perfect for Christmas. Everything was dressed in lights and the whole atmosphere was so magic.

I had bought tickets to *Mickey's Very Merry Christmas Party*, that started late in the afternoon. As soon as we came up to the main entrance—after taking the boat ride across the lake to the entrance—I saw Elsa in a holiday outfit, holding a sign for the Christmas Party. We followed her so we could enter via our special party tickets.

"*Mickey's Most Merriest Celebration* will be on the stage in front of the castle and the *Oh-so-Jolly Holiday Parade* is at six o'clock. Here's all the info you'll need," a lady wearing antlers said and handed me a brochure. "Have a great time."

The first thing I saw when we entered was Cinderella's castle, all dressed in lights, making it look like a giant ice sculpture. It was breathtaking. So were the shops and the streets, dressed in Christmas decorations. I was quickly so filled with music and Christmas spirit that I found myself pushing Sune up Main Street, humming along to Christmas carols, and eating snickerdoodle cookies. The kids walked beside me, eyes wide and mouths open, till someone handed them a cookie to stuff their mouths with. I have never seen so many cookies in my life. Or so many different types. Besides the snickerdoodles, there were snowman sugar cookies, gingersnap molasses cookies, and peppermint bark cookies. We had barely made it to the end of Main Street before William complained of a stomachache. I told Julie and Tobias to take him on a ride somewhere to get his mind off of it.

"Something gentle, not spinning too much or he might throw up," I yelled after them, but they were already gone. I had promised the big kids that if they took Will on a couple of small rides, then they could be off to the bigger ones by themselves and I would take care of Will the rest of the time.

I swallowed another cookie and washed it down with the coffee I had bought on the way. Sune seemed to enjoy his as well. I found a bench and parked him there, right in front of the castle, and we sat for a little while in silence, sipping coffee and eating cookies that were so good I was certain I would never bake any again since they would never be as moist or have the same nice texture, fluffiness, or flavor. My days as a cookie baker were over, I thought to myself with a chuckle.

Sune smiled as he spotted Donald Duck wearing a

Christmas outfit. There was a long line of kids waiting to have their pictures taken with him.

"Do you want to go see Mickey's house?" I asked. "When the kids get back?"

I felt his hand on top of mine. "I'm so glad I came."

I smiled. It was almost like seeing my old Sune again. "Well, I'm glad you did too."

"This is much better than just sitting at home all alone," he said. "So what if I have to experience it all from a chair? At least I always have somewhere to sit, right?"

The kids came back, their faces red with excitement, their hair wild. "Mom. Mom. Santa is in the Town Square," Julie said.

My heart stopped. "Really?"

"Yes," she said panting from running. "Can we take William to see him?"

"I...I..."

"Of course, you can," Sune said, looking at me annoyed. "What's wrong with you? It's Santa."

60

I followed them closely, pushing Sune in front of me.

"Why are you all worked up?" Sune asked.

"You know how I feel, Sune," I said.

"To be honest, no, I don't. I know you've told me something crazy about seeing blood in the chimney and hearing sounds coming from it. I also know you've been meeting with that detective and talked to him about some old story about a boy being trapped in the chimney and now he's haunting people or something ridiculous. What was it you said again? Oh, yeah, killing people, especially kids, all through December as a revenge. I swear, I don't know where you get all these stories from, Rebekka, but it's sounding more and more crazy and I'm getting a little worried about you."

"Right now, I'm a lot more worried about William," I said, ignoring his remarks about me being crazy.

"Well, stop it, will you? Don't ruin this trip to this

magical place by worrying about something that doesn't even exist. Please? Don't make me regret coming with you."

I sighed when I spotted Santa sitting in his sleigh in the middle of Town Square. Kids were already lining up to meet him. Including mine.

"I mean, just look at him for cryin' out loud," Sune said. "He's the merriest, jolliest fellow in the world. Look at those red cheeks, at the belly that jumps when he laughs. How can anyone be afraid of that?"

I looked at Santa sitting in his sleigh, then felt a shiver go down my spine. Was Sune right? He was the happiest guy on the planet who loved children and gave them presents. What's not to like? Why did I insist on having this dread inside of me?

"I...I just...Well, maybe this Santa is fine," I said and pushed Sune closer to make sure I was close enough to my kids to help if they needed it.

"You're darn right he's fine," Sune said with a laugh. "You worry too much, Rebekka. It's not good for you."

I drew in a deep breath of air and calmed myself down the best I knew how. The kids were so excited. I could tell by looking at their faces. Especially William. He was about to explode. Maybe I could finally get him to tell Santa what he wanted for Christmas.

"What's so creepy about him anyway?" Sune muttered.

"What's not creepy?" I asked. "I mean, come on. If anyone else acted like Santa, they'd be arrested. Think about it. He sees you when you're sleeping? The idea of an old man looming over my bed at night while I sleep isn't exactly comforting. He comes down my chimney? We let him into our houses every year and he just comes down the chimney, doesn't even use the door. He wants kids to sit on his lap? How creepy is that? He knows when I'm awake? He writes a list of people's names? Who else writes a list like that? Serial killers, that's who."

"Rebekka. You're rambling."

"I know," I said, wiping my forehead. "It's just...so many strange things have been going on lately and it's freaking me out. I'm scared, Sune."

Sune turned his head to look at me. "You're scared? That's ridiculous, Rebekka."

I nodded. "I know that's how you feel; I just can't help it after all that has been going on."

It was William's turn now and he walked to Santa and up into his sleigh where he sat on his lap, causing my heart to stop. I walked closer to see what was going on, and I heard them chatting.

"So, Will. Have you been a good boy this year?"

"Yes," Will said.

"Good. Good. And what would you like for Christmas?"

I smiled, listening in, hoping to finally figure out what to buy the boy, but then realized that whatever we bought over here would need to be transported by airplane back to Denmark. It had to fit in our suitcase.

I was afraid he might ask for a bike or something. In that case, I'd have to make up some story about his bike being at home and he'd get it when he got back. *Yes, that is it*, I thought. *I'll tell him Santa brought it to his real house. It'll work.*

But Will didn't answer. Instead, he shrugged and said: "You know what I want."

"Ho. Ho. Ho. How can I know if you don't tell me?" Santa asked.

But still, Will didn't tell him.

Santa was about to put him down when Will turned to him and asked: "Santa? Do you still have my binky?"

Santa then reached into his pocket and pulled it out. "Of course, buddy."

"Can I get it back? I miss it."

"Ho-Ho-Ho, of course, Will. Of course, you can."

61

William wanted to meet Mickey next so we took the railroad to Mickey's Toontown Fair. Tobias and Julie wanted to go to Space Mountain, so we split up once again. I was freaking out after Santa gave Will his binky back. I was in a hurry to get out of there, get away from Town Square. As we sat on the train, chugging through the Magic Kingdom, I thought I could still hear Santa laughing. It made me shiver even though it was eighty degrees.

I didn't feel like telling Sune about any of this since he was actually enjoying himself for once. I didn't want to spoil it.

We found Mickey and Minnie and got in line for a meet and greet. It took about an hour in line before it was finally William's turn, but it was worth all the wait once we got the pictures taken and to see the happy face on William.

After the photo session, we went through Mickey's

bright yellow house. It was fun for William to see his kitchen, his living room, and especially Pluto's doghouse in the yard. They had put up a Christmas tree inside Mickey's house and William and I approached it to look closer at the decorations, but then I stopped. There was a snow globe on top of the fireplace. Something was inside of it, it was snowing like someone had just shaken it, but there was something else. There was other movement inside of it. I approached it, even though Will tried to stop me, telling me I wasn't allowed to touch things. I grabbed it and held it in my hand, then nearly dropped it as I realized that inside of this globe, inside the snow, was a small Santa, waving at me. The snow in the globe soon turned red and the crimson mass ran down the glass, smearing it and making it impossible to see anything inside of it.

I gasped and put it back, then grabbed William by the hand and pulled him out of Mickey's house. Sune had already made it outside and was smiling as we got out.

"That was fun, huh, buddy?" he said to William.

"Yeah," Will said.

"I bought this for you," Sune said and handed Will a huge lollipop. It was bigger than his entire head. William lit up and grabbed it with a loud shriek.

Sune laughed. "Thought that might make you happy."

"That was nice of you," I said, still looking back over my shoulder at the house, wondering about that snow globe.

"What do you want to do next?" Sune asked, clasping his hands. "You wanna see Tomorrowland, maybe?"

William shook his head.

"All right, then how about we go see Captain Jack Sparrow at Pirates of the Caribbean?" Sune asked, sounding like a pirate by adding an *arrg* afterward.

William whined and then winced.

"He doesn't like pirates," I said. "The movies scare him."

Sune looked surprised. "Okay, then. You tell me, Will. What would you like to see next?"

"Belle's house," he said, his cheeks gleaming with joy.

Sune gave me a look. I shrugged. *Beauty and the Beast* had been Will's favorite movie for a long time, though we skipped the scary parts when the Beast fought Gaston on the roof and when he was too scary, yelling at Belle. William loved Belle and thought she was beautiful.

"Belle's house it is, I guess," Sune said as he grabbed Will and put him on his lap and rolled forward.

It warmed my heart to see the two of them together and especially seeing Sune trying so hard. William was happier than I had seen him in a very long time and I could actually say the same for Sune. This was good for them.

I looked back at Mickey's house and thought I saw something—or someone—peeking out behind the chimney. I shook my head. I simply had to keep it together. I just had to.

62

Belle's village was quaint and very much like in the movie. We started out in Maurice's cottage, the house where Belle grew up. It was a small, cute house nestled up in the woods. The inside of it could best be described as whimsical, just like Belle's father in the movie. I really enjoyed it because whoever decorated it had been very true to the movie. And that just made it even more fun for William, who knew every part of the movie by heart.

The living room surrounding the fireplace—which wasn't a real fireplace, I was happy to realize—was peppered with books, thick books, thin books, books of all colors. On the wall, they had even drawn measuring marks for Belle, where her dad supposedly had recorded her height as she grew up. William pointed at them excitedly and told me it was just like what we had on the wall at grandpa's house. He spoke while chewing on his binky and the sound made me cringe.

We walked through a door and entered Maurice's

workshop, where Maurice's many inventions were hanging or sitting everywhere, along with his tools and his drawings of upcoming inventions. William's favorite thing was a winged light fixture hanging under the ceiling; it kind of looked like Belle's dad had been inventing something that was supposed to fly but then made it into a lamp instead since he didn't want to throw anything away.

"Where is Belle?" William asked as we continued through.

"She's probably at the castle," I said, smiling. I knew there was a place where we could meet and greet Belle and decided we had to do it after this.

"Of course," Will said.

Sune told us he was feeling too hot and wanted to go outside and get some fresh air and we agreed to meet him out there, then go to the Beast's castle, and grab something to eat at the Be Our Guest Restaurant.

We stopped in front of a beautiful gilded mirror hanging on the wall. As we admired it, the mirror came alive, shining bright green, looking like pixie dust was coming off of it.

"Whoa," Will said and stepped backward.

A movie of sorts played inside the mirror, telling us this mirror was a portal, taking us now to the castle. In the mirror's movie, we flew across the forest and could see the castle in the distance, then stopped at the front door. The mirror told us we were about to meet the first friend Belle ever made at the castle and that was when the movie stopped.

William shrieked.

"What happened, Mommy? Where's the wardrobe? I want to see the wardrobe; where is she?"

"I...I guess the movie is over," I said, just as something else came onto the screen. Something far more terrifying than the sweet opera-singing wardrobe from the movie.

"Mommy? Is that...Santa?"

I gasped and pulled my son back, away from the mirror.

"Let's get out of here," I said as the grinning face approached us and poked his entire head out of the screen, staring down at us, laughing so loud it bounced off of the brick walls surrounding us.

"Mommy?" William said, his voice shaking. "Why does Santa have such long teeth?"

"I don't know, sweetie," I said, looking around the room, my eyes settling on some of Maurice's tools, wondering if they were real and if I could pick them up in case it became necessary.

"Mommy? Why are Santa's eyes so red?"

"I...I don't know that either, Will."

Santa poked out his hand toward us, reaching for us, when William asked, his voice shivering:

"Mommy? Why does Santa have such long dirty nails? And why is he looking at us the way he is?"

I felt the panic rush through me but stood as if paralyzed. I backed up slowly, pulling Will with me, grabbing the door handle behind me, turning it, fumbling for a firm grasp on the knob, my hand slipping because it was wet with sweat. As I managed to get a firmer grasp on it and tried to turn it, the door didn't open. Turning the knob more frantically didn't help. I closed my eyes, panic rising in my mind, threatening to spill over. I fought against it and stood there perfectly still, holding my son like a statue with a pulse pounding in its throat.

Crazily, I thought, *I could call for help.*

But who would come? Who would believe me? Who would make it in time?

I put the back of my hand up to my mouth and bit down on it. I tried to think, to push back the panic of my beating heart and just think.

But all that came to my mind were images of Sydney, her chest ripped open, and of Sara—poor Sara Andrews—dangling from a string of Christmas lights. And for now, all I could do was simply stand still, hands tightly wrapped around my son, my face alarmed, my eyes beginning to bulge.

"I'm scared, Mommy!"

Will was chewing his pacifier loudly. I felt my nostrils flaring and the sides of my mouth pulling down into a dreadful grimace of horror. My brain wanted to scream, to shout, to call for someone to come, but I couldn't.

William was whimpering. I could feel his small body bouncing between my hands. I tried to turn the knob behind me again, first to one side, then the other.

Santa was grinning, approaching William, reaching out his long nails toward him, his red glowing eyes set on the boy. His breath smelled like candy when he spoke, his voice hissing, yet alluring.

"W-i-i-i-li-a-am. Come to Santa, William. Santa will grant you a-a-all your wishes. Have you been a goo-oo-ood boy, huh, William? Or have you been NAUGHTY?"

"Mommy! Mommy! Mommy! MOMMY!"

Frantically, I pulled the knob and shook the door behind me. I turned around and knocked on it, hard, panicking as I slammed my fists into it, when it was suddenly opened from the outside and I rushed out, William's hand in mine with William crying and screaming.

63

"Daddy, Daddy, Daddy, it was awful!"

William ran to Sune and threw himself in his lap. Sune looked at me, then down at the boy.

"What's going on? Buddy? Are you okay? What happened?"

"We have to get out of here," I said and grabbed Sune's chair and started to push him, rushing out of Belle's village, out of Fantasyland.

"Where are we going, Rebekka?" Sune asked.

People were jumping out of the way to not get hit by the wheelchair; some complained and yelled at us angrily, but I didn't care. My heart was still pounding loudly and I had to get away, as far away from this place as possible.

We slowed down in front of Prince Charming's Carousel. William sniffled and started begging to go on the carousel, so I told him I would go on the ride with him.

Sune grabbed my hand as we were leaving to get in line.

"What the heck is going on, Rebekka? What happened inside that house? What scared him so much?"

I really didn't want to talk about it, but he deserved an explanation. I drew in a deep breath, wondering what to tell him. I knew he would never believe me if I told him the truth.

Will threw me under the bus.

"Santa," he said, still chewing on his pacifier. "Scary Santa."

Sune's eyes grew wide. "Again with the Santa? Why are you filling him with all this nonsense, Rebekka? You're completely ruining Christmas for him. Now he's scared of Santa? You did that to him, Rebekka. You're the one filling him with all this stuff."

"Carousel, carousel," Will begged, pulling my hand.

I didn't want to fight with Sune anymore, so I just turned my back on him and followed my son into the line. It didn't take long before I was sitting on a horse, Will on the one next to me, seemingly already forgetting everything. If only I had the mind of a child. I, for one, couldn't shake the experience and the dread was still inside of me, my hands still shaking. It couldn't have been just an illusion, could it? William saw it too. Just like the big kids had seen the blood in the chimney, but Sune hadn't seen any of it.

Because you'll start believing in him. He only comes to those who believe

Those had been the words of Sara Andrews. She had

warned me. She had told me that if she told me her story, I would start believing he was real, that this terrible version of our beloved jolly Santa was real. And so, he would come for me. Was that what had happened to Dr. Hahn? To Sydney's dad?

Sune hasn't seen him. He hasn't heard the stories, so he doesn't believe it.

I realized that Sune's ignorance and ability to refuse to believe what I told him were actually what was saving him from also entering this nightmare. It was what was keeping him safe. I didn't need to convince him that it was real; I needed him to convince me it wasn't.

The carousel spun around and around, faster and faster, and I enjoyed the wind on my face, trying to let this entire experience dissipate from my memory, shaking it, letting the crazy pitchy carousel music into my mind, letting it take over while replacing all the bad thoughts with good ones, as the horse went up and down.

Up and down.

64

As I GOT off the carousel, William's hand in mine, Julie and Tobias came running up to us.

"Mom, the *Oh-so-Jolly Holiday Parade* is about to start," she said. "We need to get a good spot."

I kissed my daughter and held her close.

"Mom, what's the matter?"

I shook my head. "Nothing. I just missed you. That's all. Did you have fun on the rides?"

"Yes," Julie said. "Tobias and I went on everything. Space Mountain is sooo much fun. You should try it, Mom."

I laughed. "I think I'm a little too old for that."

"Here they come," Tobias said.

The loud music drowned out everything else, as the parade approached us in a sea of lights. People gathered around us and soon we were standing very close. A lady next to me held up her phone to make a video while dancing and I wondered what kind of video she would end up with.

"There's Donald Duck," Will exclaimed. He started to wave and Donald waved back while dancing down the street to the most joyful Christmas music.

"And Chip and Dale," Tobias said and waved. The chipmunks waved back.

"And Elsa!" Julie said, sounding a little more excited than she wanted to as the entire cast of *Frozen* filed by.

"BELLE!" William gave me a blissful smile as his favorite princess showed up, riding on a float made from a giant stack of books.

A set of trumpet-and-drum-playing toy soldiers followed, along with reindeer and Goofy, Minnie, and finally a Christmas-dressed Mickey Mouse. The kids waved and danced to the music, while I took pictures with my phone. It was truly spectacular and everything I had hoped it would be.

It had gotten dark out and the parade glittered beautifully in the darkness. Fake snow was falling from the lampposts in a bluish light. People on skis, with wheels underneath, rushed by, pretending to be skiing. And then came Olaf to the tune of *Let It Snow*. Olaf giggled loudly, then passed us.

"Pluto!" Will said.

"Peter Pan," Tobias said.

"Winnie the Pooh," Julie said.

"Santa!" Sune said and pointed.

I stopped waving and froze as the float carrying Santa came toward us in the distance. He was sitting in a huge sleigh, reindeer and elves dancing in front of it,

Christmas lights glowing around it. Bells were ringing, loud jingle bells, and Santa was waving from atop it. The music shifted to *Santa Claus is Coming to Town* and all the kids around us cheered.

Except William.

He backed up into my arms and hid.

"Here comes Santa Claus, Here comes Santa Claus," they all chanted.

Sune was probably the loudest of them all. He was so happy, singing along, getting Julie and Tobias to sing as well. Meanwhile, I could feel William's small hand shaking in mine.

65

The sight of Santa was scaring me but I felt safe with all these people around me. Yet, I kept William close as the float filed by us, Santa waving and laughing merrily from it.

Julie and Tobias waved back eagerly and Santa looked down at them, holding his belly and waving back.

I held my breath as he passed William and me, then finally breathed freely as it was almost past us and Santa focused on what was ahead, on the kids standing next to us.

And then he turned his head.

I gasped and backed up into someone standing behind me, pulling William with me. Santa's red glowing eyes were on us now, and he was smiling that awful smile of his behind the thick beard, showing off his pointy teeth.

"M-mommy?" Will said.

"Let's get out of here," I said and elbowed myself out

of the crowd. With Will's hand in mine, I walked fast away from the parade, away from the crowd and the loud noise, my heart pounding in my chest.

"Peter Pan!" Will said happily and pointed at a small roller coaster ride behind us called Peter Pan's Flight.

I stared at the parade and Santa disappearing. "You wanna go on that? We can do that," I said and hurried to the entrance of it before everyone else came from watching the parade and created a line. I texted Sune and let him know where we were.

Will and I were the first to get in. We found a carriage and sat down and a second later the ride began. William was still shaking as we took off into the world of Peter Pan, starting in the bedroom where Wendy and her siblings were getting ready for bed. It was a very sweet and quiet ride and soon it made me relax and breathe normally again. Next, we were pulled upward and flew above the housetops, floating like we were flying with Peter Pan. William sucked his pacifier and looked down, pointing.

"Grandpa."

"You think grandpa is living down there," I said with a chuckle. I realized I missed him terribly and wondered if he was all right, while flying in our little carriage above the Thames, Big Ben beneath us.

"Neverland," William said dreamily and pointed as the landscape below us changed to cliffs and lakes.

"Pirates," he said, concerned, when we spotted a pirate ship. Will lifted his arm, his eyebrows wrinkled. "Hook."

"I know," I said looking behind me to make sure Santa hadn't followed us in here. There was no one in the seats in front of us or behind us. There was nothing to worry about. I turned back to look at the scenery in front of us.

"Captain Hook. That's him right there, see? He's fighting with someone. Who's he fighting with, Will?"

William smiled widely. "Peter Pan!"

Hook and Pan were rocking back and forth in the old display of them in a sword battle on top of the pirate ship, balancing on the boom. It was cute and a little amusing.

"Don't like Hook," Will said, shaking his head.

"You don't like Hook? Well, no one likes him, I guess."

"I'll get you, Peter Pan," Hook yelled over the speakers and they kept fighting, when suddenly Hook stopped what he was doing and jumped out of the scenery, onto our carriage.

His red eyes glowed at us as he swung his hook at us, yelling: "What do you want for Christmas, Will, what do you want? What do you want? Huh? Huh?"

66

THE HOOK SWUNG above my head just as I ducked, and it slammed into the pole behind me. William screamed. I grabbed him in my arms and ducked again as the hook once again came toward me.

"Mommy!"

"We gotta get out of this ride," I said and was about to jump out, when suddenly the carriage moved faster, spinning out of control. I was thrown back in the seat as the exhibition rushed past us, the carriage going faster and faster. I was screaming at the top of my lungs and William was as well. We came close to the exit, but the ride didn't stop, it just hurried past the platform where all the next guests were waiting to get in, then rushed back inside the ride once again. People screamed and so did I. Still, the wagon was accelerating, going faster than any roller coaster I had ever been in.

"Stop it, Mommy! Make it stop," Will cried.

Meanwhile, Hook, who had now turned into Santa—yet still with the hook for a hand—was sitting above us on the plastic carriage's boom, laughing, yelling out into the air.

"Tell me what you want for Christmas, Will!!"

Once again, we rushed past the entire exhibition, then out to the outside where people were still screaming as we rushed past them back inside, where the ride continued all over.

"Stop it," I cried. "Just make it stop."

Santa jumped into the carriage, sitting in the seats in front of us, looking back at us, smirking, showing off his spiky teeth. He was giggling.

"I brought your little friend," he said.

In front of me sat Sydney. My heart literally stopped, but as I looked at her, I realized it wasn't really her. Her eyes were different.

"I love Christmas," she said. "It's my favorite time of year. Where I am now it's Christmas all year around. Doesn't that sound like FUN?"

I looked behind her and saw Tobin, Dr. Hahn, the girl from the carol singing choir, along with hundreds of other dead faces sitting inside the carriages, riding the ride. I could hear them singing Christmas carols.

I was breathing in short shallow gasps as I watched Sydney's face disappear and Santa return. He was laughing as we rushed toward the exit once again, passed the crowd outside, and back inside the ride. I wondered if it would ever stop. I felt so nauseous, it almost hurt.

Santa held the hook out in front of us, then swung it once again, missing my head by an inch. I gasped and ducked down to the bottom of the carriage, pulling Will with me. Santa was laughing above us. I heard his boots land next to us inside the carriage, closed my eyes, and prepared for it all to be over. The hook hit me first on the arm, penetrated the skin and went in deep, blood spurting out. I screamed when suddenly the carriage stopped abruptly. Santa was swung over the edge and flew onto the tracks. The wagon then started to back up, going back outside where a crowd had gathered. Two security guards helped us get out and some official representing Disney came up to us. He looked like he was fifteen.

"I am so sorry, ma'am. I can't tell you how awful we all feel. This has never happened before."

He looked at my arm. It was bleeding heavily. "Oh, my," he said. "Do you want us to take you to see a medical professional? We have paramedics waiting right down here."

I nodded, unable to speak. Will was clinging to my leg.

I spotted Sune in front of us, rolling closer, his face concerned. "What happened?"

I scoffed, then shook my head and let the paramedic attend to my wound.

"The ride got stuck somehow," the official person explained. "We will, of course, have to close it down till we figure out what happened. And you'll get compensation. And free annual passes, naturally."

I didn't care much about what the man said. My heart was still pounding in my chest, but I didn't want to tell Sune anything. I just wanted to get out of there, fast.

67

I HAD to have stitches in my arm to close up the wound, so they took me to the nearest emergency room and patched me up. It was painful, but to be honest, the worst part was all the waiting.

Before they could release me, I had to sign a ton of papers stating I wasn't going to sue Disney World. When I was finally done, I found the kids and Sune waiting for me in the lobby of the hospital.

The kids all hugged me and Julie asked if my arm was okay. I told her it would be. Will was more concerned about me being able to unwrap presents for Christmas.

We drove back toward Cocoa Beach. No one spoke for the longest part of the ride, except for a few sentences about how good it was going to be to get back home and how we really needed a quiet night's sleep.

My arm hurt but I could still drive and I just wanted to get back to the beach house and as far away from Disney World and Orlando as possible. The kingdom didn't seem so magical to me anymore. Neither did Florida or Cocoa Beach, for that matter. I just really missed home.

I had called my dad from the hospital to tell him what had happened. I didn't go into detail but explained that I had been in an accident and that I was getting stitches. He wasn't feeling well, he said. The nurse said he had a bladder infection again, but it was really hurting this time, he said. I was worried about him. And I felt terrible for abandoning him at Christmas. Who knew if it would be his last?

We entered the beach house and I dropped my backpack on the floor, then threw myself on the couch. William had slept in the car, so he was awake now and wanted to watch a movie. Against my better judgment, but in order to have a little peace and quiet, I put on *Beauty and the Beast*. The big kids went on their computers upstairs before bedtime and, to my surprise, Sune didn't retract to the media room, but rolled up next to the couch and sat with us, while being on his iPad.

It didn't take ten seconds before I dozed off. I dreamt about my dad and that I was with him again. I don't know exactly where we were, but I was holding his hand while he was lying in his bed, breathing with difficulty. I was worried about him, worried he was going to die, asking him what I was supposed to do without him. Then, for some reason, my mom was suddenly there, even though she had been dead for many years. I spoke to her about my dad and she told me he was going to Disney World soon.

I woke up with a gasp, my heart beating fast, worrying it was some sort of premonition, that soon my mom and dad would be in the same place, a sort of heavenly Disney World—which to me right now sounded more like hell—when my phone buzzed on the table in front of me. I grabbed it and looked at the display, blinking my eyes to better focus.

It was a text from Alyssa.

I CAN HEAR HIM. HE'S OUTSIDE MY ROOM. HIS NAILS ARE SCRAPING ON MY DOOR. I AM ALONE. MOM AND DAD ARE OUT. PLEASE, HELP ME!

68

I RAN AS FAST as I could down the beach till I found Alyssa's house. Panting, my legs hurting from running, I stopped on the porch outside and looked up at the chimney where I remembered they had pulled out Tobin on the first day I was here. I swallowed hard, then rushed to the sliding doors and pulled them open.

As I walked into the living room and across the carpet, I could hear the chimney. It was like it was calling to me, a pulse pounding inside of it. I stopped and stared at it, my heart in my throat. Blood was running down the walls of the brick fireplace in long thin stripes.

I heard a sound. It was coming from upstairs.

I ran up and found Alyssa's room. The door wasn't knocked in, it was ripped to pieces. I stepped over the broken wood. Inside the room, I found Alyssa. She was not on her bed but hung up against the wall above her bed, a belt around her throat, a thick black leather belt with a solid brass buckle. Her face was purple, her screams caught in her throat.

"Alyssa," I said as I ran to her, unfastened the belt, and let her fall to the bed.

"Are you all right?" I asked.

She fought to speak but had no breath. The belt had left deep bruises on her throat. She was coughing and panting, getting her breath back, crawling on all fours, throwing up on the bed.

"He ripped the door," she said between moans. "Clawed his way through."

"Are you hurt anywhere else?" I asked.

She shook her head, struggling to swallow, putting a hand to her throat. She coughed again, snot coming from her nose, saliva running from her mouth onto the bedspread.

Why hadn't he killed her? Why hadn't he given her the red marks? Was he in a hurry? Did I scare him away?

"Maybe he had something else planned," I mumbled.

"What?" Alyssa asked, finally able to speak almost normally.

My heart dropped as the realization sunk in. My eyes grew wide and I looked at Alyssa.

"Will."

"What are you talking about?"

"He wanted me out of the house," I said, gasping for air as my throat was narrowing, panic erupting like waves in my body. "He's been after Will all this time."

69

His dad had fallen asleep, but William wasn't tired. Not at all. He had slept in the car and he didn't need any more sleep. But his movie was done and his mom gone and now Will had no idea what to do next.

He heard a rustle coming from the Christmas tree in the corner and decided to go check it out. He wondered if it might be a squirrel or a bird or something fun like in the trees outside. He wasn't going to miss out on that.

Will approached the Christmas tree and laughed when he saw his own reflection in the globes, his face all deformed and funny. Will reached up and grabbed a globe between his chubby little fingers, then pulled it off the tree and looked into it. He liked the way binky looked in it when he sucked on it and laughed again. Then he tilted his head as he saw something else in it, something that looked like it was coming up behind him. Remembering the bad Santa he had seen at Disney World earlier in the day, Will threw the globe onto the tiles. The globe didn't shatter, but bounced right back up, making a funny noise, and soon Will had forgotten all about what he had seen inside of it and was chasing the globe through the living room, bouncing it off the tiles like a ball, giggling his little heart out.

When he got to the chimney, he stopped and forgot all about the globe. He was chewing his pacifier while staring at the white brick fireplace in front of him. He wasn't staring at it because it was in any way funny or interesting. No, he was staring because he could hear something. It was coming from inside of it. A sound.

The sound of nails scraping against a wall.

Will didn't understand how such a sound could come from inside the chimney and for a while he stared at it, quite fascinated and a little frightened.

When the scraping suddenly turned into a voice, he felt safer. The voice was calling his name, whispering it, sounding like the wind blowing. Then, seconds later, a face peeked out from inside the chimney. It was facing upside down.

"Hello, Will," it said.

Will stood still, chewing on his pacifier. Will might only have been four years old, but he still knew a bad Santa when he saw one. And this was the one. This was the very same one he had seen earlier in the day, the one trying to hurt his mother with his hook. Will was not happy to see this bad Santa here in his house and, to be honest, it scared him, a lot.

The bearded man in the chimney peeking out smiled, then, suddenly, he was gone. Will gasped and stared at the spot where the face had been, then gasped once again, a little startled when the face came back, only to be gone a second later.

Then Will giggled. He knew this game. His mom played it with him often and both of them would always squeal with joy.

Santa was back and then gone again. Then he came back and was gone once again. Will's giggles turned into laughter and he forgot all about bad Santa and approached the chimney, trying to catch him as he disappeared again.

Where did he go?

"Peek a boo," Santa said and peeked his head out again.

Will laughed. He reached out to grab Santa, but he was gone again.

"Huh?" Will said looking at his empty hands, then at the chimney in front of him.

Where did he go?

Will heard a sound from inside the chimney, then decided he had to go up there. He crawled up into the fireplace, pulled himself inside, then peeked up into the chimney, trying hard to see Santa peeking inside the darkness. He reached his hand up to see if he could feel him, when the bad Santa grabbed his arm and held it tight, then pulled the boy up into the chimney.

70

I stormed down the beach. It was dark, so I didn't see the smoke coming from our chimney till I was on the porch. My heart literally stopped. I stormed inside the sliding doors. As I entered, I could hear what sounded like laughter, a deep rolling laughter.

The fire was lit in the fireplace. I ran to the kitchen, grabbed the fire extinguisher, and put it out. The fire spurted and fought back, but soon died. I then climbed inside, on top of the white foam, and looked up. I could see Will's little foot. I reached inside, grabbed him by the heel, and pulled. He didn't come down. He didn't even move. He was stuck and not moving.

This wasn't good.

Images of Tobin being pulled out of the fireplace, lifeless, emerged violently and made me cry in desperation. My cries awoke Sune.

"What's going on, Rebekka?" he asked and rolled

slowly toward us, looking like he believed he was still dreaming.

"It's Will," I said, my voice breaking. "He's stuck. Inside the ch-ch-chimney."

"Oh, dear God," Sune said, his voice desperate. "How the heck did he get up there?"

"I don't know," I said. "I'm trying to get him down but he's not moving. I'm afraid of hurting him."

"Try to grab both his feet and wiggle him slightly," Sune said, rolling his chair closer. "I'll call 911."

I tried. The boy moved a little but it wasn't enough to get him down. My arm was hurting and I had to stop pulling. "I can't," I said.

"The kids," Sune said, then rolled to the stairs. "Julie, Tobias!"

They rushed down to us, their eyes concerned.

"It's Will," I said. "He's stuck. We can't get him out. You're smaller."

"Let me," Julie said and stepped forward. She crawled into the fireplace, stuck her head up in the chimney, grabbed Will's leg further up, and pulled, hard. I cringed, worrying both that Julie might get hurt and that all that pulling might hurt William.

"Argh," she said. "He's stuck."

"Try wiggling him a little," Sune said.

Julie did. "He's still not coming down."

Julie came out and I went back inside to try again. I sensed Julie had made him looser and he was easier to wiggle now. I pulled his leg but still nothing. I screamed in frustration, knowing my boy was probably getting suffocated up there. I started to cry, then screamed again in anger, grabbed both of my boy's legs, and pulled with all my might, yelling and screaming, not caring that my arm hurt like crazy and the stitches were coming loose, springing like buttons on a shirt ripped open. Blood was gushing out from my wound, but my boy was moving, slowly coming loose. I panted and laughed as his small body came closer and closer, and soon fell into my painful arms.

Julie came to fetch him and pull him out, and I was about to get out myself, when suddenly something reached down from inside the chimney behind me, grabbed my ankle, and pulled me up forcefully.

71

I was screaming and kicking. Outside the chimney, I could hear the kids' terrified screams. Whatever was pulling me was very strong and I went into the chimney fast, hitting my head on the soot-covered sides. I was pulled up far, so far that I could no longer see the bottom, then the pulling stopped and I realized I was stuck. Whatever had grabbed my foot now let go, and I couldn't move. My wound had opened further and blood gushed out of it, dripping down into the fireplace beneath me. I was starting to feel dizzy, maybe from losing blood or maybe from the lack of air inside the chimney. I felt like I could hardly breathe.

A face appeared beneath me. The face of Santa crawling up toward me, his long arms and legs clinging to the sides of the brick chimney like a daddy longlegs spider.

"Let me go," I said. "Please."

"Sorry," Santa said, grinning, rushing toward me. "No can do. No can do. No can do. No, ma'am."

He was right in front of me, opening his mouth, his red eyes glowing in the darkness, lighting up the chimney with a creepy red light, his teeth glistening in that light, his long sharp teeth. He was grinning from ear to ear, moving so close I could smell him now, smell his minty candy cane breath.

He crawled up to me, spotted the bare skin on my neck, and leaned over. I felt his teeth as they pricked against my skin when suddenly there was an earthquake. The entire chimney shook and then it exploded. Exploded in a mass of bricks and dirt and soot all around me and I started to fall toward the ground. I screamed and landed on top of a pile of bricks. Then I felt hands on me and was pulled out of it.

When I came to myself, the first thing I saw was Julie holding Will in her arms. He was awake and clinging to his big sister. Next, I spotted Sune, the ax from the garage in his hand. He was in a fight with Santa, who was growling and snapping his teeth at him, crawling around on his long skinny arms and legs.

Sune swung the ax and hit the monster right in his throat, chopping his head off, and it flew across the living room. All the kids screamed while Sune jumped to avoid being struck by Santa's long nails, as he was still moving, despite the chopped off head.

Sune swung the ax once again and split the Santa right down the middle, then swung it again and again till Santa was nothing but chopped up pieces, hissing and growling as they lay on the carpet, slowly fading out, becoming colorless, then turning to dust, a dust that soon dissipated completely.

I swallowed hard and looked at Sune as he was panting, yet, triumphantly, he looked at me with the ax still between his hands.

"Sune," I said.

He looked at me.

"You're standing. On your feet."

As I said it, Sune realized what had happened and sunk to the ground, landing on his knees. The kids ran to him and carried him back up into his chair. "I...I didn't think," he said. "I just got so scared and sprang for the ax when you were pulled up into that thing. Then I started to tear it down. I'm so sorry I didn't believe you, Rebekka. I'm so, so sorry."

"It's okay," I said. "I think you killed it. I think it's gone now. We did it, Sune. You and me, babe."

He laughed and the kids joined us in a major group hug.

EPILOGUE

CHAPTER 72

Christmas Eve, we ate our duck dinner, the way Danish people do, and danced around the Christmas tree. Sune took one round with us, supported by me till he could stand no more and had to get back to his chair. Since the night when we had killed the monster in the living room, we had visited with doctor Herman again and told him how Sune had suddenly gotten out of his chair when realizing he had no choice, and the doctor had nodded happily and told us this was exactly what he had been waiting for. He also said that with the rate things were going, he was certain he could have Sune walking within the next year. If Sune kept improving the way he was.

But that meant he had to come in several times a week for training and that also meant we had to stay here in Florida. I had called home and talked to Jens-Ole. He had told me he could allow for me to take a year of leave, but I had to promise that I would come back because he couldn't run the paper without me.

"We have no stories when you're gone, Rebekka. I don't know what to put in the paper."

I made the promise, then hung up, wondering if I could get a job over here writing for some magazine. Or maybe another European paper would hire me to write stories over here. So far, I had managed to sell the story of the killer-Santa to a paranormal magazine here in the States and the money I got from that would help us out for a couple of weeks. There was also the issue of visas if we were going to stay here for more than three months. And if I was going to work, I needed a work visa.

Finally, there was the issue of my dad. He had given us his blessing to stay but told us he wouldn't be able to come and be with us since there was no way he would be able to cope with the long flight. I promised I would come visit often and bring the kids as often as I could.

There were a lot of things I would have to look into as soon as Christmas was over, but for now, I was determined to enjoy my holiday with my family and especially with Sune, who was getting closer to getting back to being himself. He had regained hope, and hope was everything.

He smiled and kissed me, then sat down while the rest of us continued the caroling and dancing, hand in hand around the tree. William soon got tired of the dancing too and sat on his father's lap, while the big kids and I sang one more song before we gave in too and sat down.

We looked at the beautiful tree in front of us and then at the broken chimney next to it. There were still bricks all over the floor and soot and dirt, but we had managed to gather it all into a pile while waiting for the owners to fix it. So far, they had covered the open parts of it with a tarp. I had put in a request to stay for a longer period of time, but they hadn't answered yet. I was hoping that us destroying the chimney wasn't going to be a problem. We had promised we'd pay for it.

As is the Danish tradition, the kids received their presents on Christmas Eve, and they started to unwrap them. William shrieked with joy when he found his iPhone. Yes, I had caved and bought him one, under the condition that he gave me the pacifier and never asked for it back. He had finally agreed to it, and now he was staring at the new phone between his hands with gleaming eyes. I felt like a terrible mother for letting my young boy have a phone, but no one is perfect, right?

I, for one, am not.

William thanked me and kissed me when I heard caroling coming from outside. I opened the door and found detective Jack Ryder along with what I could only assume had to be his wife and five children. I had heard that he was married to some famous country singer, but since I wasn't into that type of music, I couldn't tell her apart from anyone else, but I could hear that she sang beautifully.

"Merry Christmas," Jack Ryder said when the song was over. "We're trying out a new tradition, singing to people in the neighborhood to spread a little Christmas cheer."

"It was very beautiful," I said. I hesitated for just a second, then added: "Don't you want to come in?"

Jack and his wife looked at one another, then she shrugged.

"Why not?"

I looked at Sune to make sure it was okay and he nodded. "Yes, come on inside. We have loads of cookies and candy."

Jack Ryder smiled, ran a hand through his long blond hair, and they came inside. I had met up with him during the week and told him the entire story. He had even read my article. I wasn't sure he believed it fully, but I still had the stitches in my arm to prove it. I didn't need him to believe me to know what happened. I still shivered when thinking about it.

"This is Shannon," Jack said and pointed at the beautiful woman that he was obviously very proud to be with.

I shook her hand. "Good to meet you," I said. "Now, you'll have to please excuse us, but the living room is quite a mess. Our chimney sort of broke."

"Then Santa won't be able to find you?" one of Jack's twins, Austin said, slightly worried.

I looked at him and smiled.

"We sure hope not," I said, closing the front door. "We sure hope not."

THE END

Want to know Sara Andrews' story, as she told it to Dr. Hahn?

Get *Better Watch Out* here:
http://amzn.to/2iE3xny

AFTERWORD

Dear Reader,

Thank you for purchasing *Better Not Cry*. For those of you who haven't read *Better Watch Out*, this story is sort of a sequel to that one. It is a short story featuring Sara Andrews telling her story to Dr. Hahn. It was while writing the short story that I came up with the idea to continue this storyline in a real novel. Also, because so many of you readers asked me to tell more.

Now, the idea of a bad Santa or Santa being evil came from my two young girls. They used to always say they found Santa very creepy, with him looking at us while we're sleeping and all. And once we went to the mall and there was a Santa there and we got up to him and they sat on his lap. In the end, he wanted them to kiss him on his cheeks while Mrs. Claus took pictures of them that we could buy afterward. Both the girls and I found it a little too creepy and I knew I had to write about it one day.

Afterword

It was fun to write about Rebekka again and I guess she and her family will be in Florida for a little while. And now they are becoming friends with Jack Ryder and his family. I have a feeling we might see more of that combination in the future.

As always, I am grateful for all your support. Don't forget to leave a review if you can.

Take care,

Willow

ABOUT THE AUTHOR

The Queen of Scream, Willow Rose, is an international best-selling author. She writes Mystery/Suspense/Horror, Paranormal Romance and Fantasy. She is inspired by authors like James Patterson, Agatha Christie, Stephen King, Anne Rice, and Isabel Allende. She lives on Florida's Space Coast with her husband and two daughters. When she is not writing or reading, you'll find her surfing and watching the dolphins play in the waves of the Atlantic Ocean. She has sold more than two million books.

To be the first to hear about new releases and bargains—from Willow Rose—sign up below to be on the VIP List. (I promise not to share your email with anyone else, and I won't clutter your inbox.)

- Sign up to be on the VIP LIST here :
http://eepurl.com/wcGej

Connect with Willow online:
willow-rose.net
madamewillowrose@gmail.com

GIRL DIVIDED, EXCERPT

For a special sneak peak of Willow Rose's Bestselling post-apocalyptic Novel ***Girl Divided*** turn to the next page.

THEY THINK SHE'S A MONSTER. BUT SHE'S THEIR ONLY HOPE...

GIRL DIVIDED

AMAZON #1 BEST SELLING AUTHOR

WILLOW ROSE

PROLOGUE

CHAPTER 1

Even the people starting the fire probably could never foresee the havoc and destruction it would cause. Maybe they could and maybe they wanted it. Maybe that was why they did it. But, then again, do people really want war? Or does it just happen?

The people of the Calvary Temple Baptist Church, who met in the red wooden building on Alvin Callender Street in the heart of New Orleans, certainly never thought of this bright and unusually hot Sunday morning as a turning point in history when they arrived at church just before ten o'clock as usual.

To them, it was a Sunday like every other.

Well, that isn't entirely the truth. Something was very different this morning, something that had all the church-goers' attention, but it wasn't something they spoke about out loud. Instead, they whispered as they passed, or stared at Tiffany from the pews in front of her with curious eyes and some anxiety.

Tiffany knew they were staring and whispering behind her back, but she cared very little. She loved her newborn baby girl, no matter if people talked and whispered about her freakish appearance. It was, after all, not her fault that she looked the way she did.

How could anyone act like this toward a young child?

Next to Tiffany sat Gregory, her husband. He was sighing and rubbing his forehead, partly because of the heat, but mostly because he was not enjoying the many stares and glances falling upon him, wondering, *could he really be the father? How could they have had a little girl like that, being as they were both black? How had they had a child that was half white and half of color?*

But the child was his. Tiffany had assured him repeatedly. She had not been with another man. No one could explain why the girl looked like this. Not even the doctors. Maybe it was a lack of melanin, they stated. But no one knew for certain what caused it. There had been records of children with one blue and one brown eye before, but never of one having one entire side of their face and body white, the skin and hair as white as snow, and the other side black and dark as the night.

But that was the way Jetta was. And Tiffany loved her just the same.

"Let's close our eyes and pray," Pastor Lawrence said.

Tiffany did, holding baby Jetta close to her chest while she slept. Only three weeks old and she was the dearest thing. Tiffany had heard so many stories of how the baby would ruin her sleep, but there had been nothing of that sort from Jetta. She had been sleeping...

well, like a baby...ever since birth and never fussed much. The quietness along with her appearance had made Tiffany's mother anxious.

"The child is evil, I tell ya," she said, spitting on the floor. She was trying to drive out the demon in her whenever Tiffany wasn't looking. "I can smell it on her skin. Death and decay from the pit of hell. Still smells burnt. She is sent here to destroy us all, I tell ya."

"She is no such thing," Tiffany had told her, laughing even though she was slightly anxious. Her mother had always believed in all that old superstition. Growing up in New Orleans, Tiffany had listened to it all her life. All the nonsense about the spirits and gods walking among us, but Tiffany never quite bought into any of it. Still, when you have listened to things like that your entire life, you never can stop wondering, *what if? What if there is something to what she is saying?*

"Nonsense," Tiffany had told her repeatedly. Not just to convince her mother, but also her worried self.

"It's just superstition."

But her mother wouldn't stop. Just this morning, before church, her old mother had looked her straight in the eyes and said:

"This child is a sign that darker times are ahead. I am tellin' you, darker times are ahead of us."

Luckily, Gregory was a Christian and he had taken Tiffany to church once they met, and there, she had finally found something she could believe in: Love. Nothing else. No dancing spirits or darkness lurking around every street corner. Just peace and love. Tiffany refused to let her mother destroy the happiest moment of her entire life by worrying about something so silly.

Jetta made a sound and Tiffany chuckled. Gregory grabbed her hand and squeezed it while Pastor Lawrence spoke.

They didn't even hear the doors being locked from the outside.

CHAPTER 2

The smell was the first thing they noticed. The smell of smoke. Gregory was the first to react. He sniffed the air and looked at Tiffany.

"Do you smell smoke?"

She lifted her nose, then shook her head. "No."

Jetta had opened her eyes and was looking up at her mother. Tiffany's arm was getting tired from holding the baby, but she didn't want to put her down. She was afraid she might cry. Not that she ever cried, at least not yet, but it sure would be bad timing if she started now.

Tiffany chuckled again when her eyes met Jetta's. Such an intense glare from such a small creature. Tiffany couldn't take her eyes off her. She was no longer listening to Pastor Lawrence's preaching - not that she ever really did, as she usually would doze off about halfway through his sermon.

"Okay, good," Gregory said and let it go.

But only for a few minutes. Until someone sitting

closer to the door smelled it too. Soon, people were asking other people sitting next to them if they smelled smoke too, and they did. Tiffany smelled it too and soon her blissful smile turned into one of anxiety. Gregory rose to his feet and looked at the pastor.

"Lawrence, I think we need to get people out of here."

But it was too late. The sound of the flames licking the sides of the church was suddenly deafening and Tiffany felt panic rise, not just in her, but also in everyone inside the small building. It rushed through them like a blazing wave.

"FIRE!" someone yelled when she spotted smoke seeping in from under the door.

Screams emerged and people rushed to the doors leading outside. Gregory was in front, making sure Tiffany and the baby were protected from the stampede. He grabbed the handle and shook it, but the door didn't open.

"It's locked," he said.

"Try the emergency exits," Pastor Lawrence said and pointed to both sides, where exit signs were lit up.

It was already getting hotter inside the church and Tiffany felt her heart thump in her chest as she rushed—along with everyone else—toward the exit doors, but as someone grabbed the doors, they couldn't open them either. None of them.

They were trapped.

Tiffany turned her head and looked at Gregory for help. "It's locked, Greg. What are we going to do?"

He looked around, sweat trickling from his forehead.

The place was an old movie theater; there were no windows they could crawl out of, no other way out but the doors.

"We're gonna die," some old lady in a pink dress screamed. "We're all gonna die!"

Pastor Lawrence grabbed a chair and threw it at the door, but it just bounced back from the heavy door. He rubbed his head as the entire congregation looked at him for help. Meanwhile, the heat grew stronger...on the verge of unbearable.

"I...I don't know what to do," he said.

Gregory grabbed his cellphone. "I'll call for help," he said. "I'm calling 911 now."

As Gregory spoke to the dispatcher, the fire had already reached the roof, and flaming pieces of the ceiling were falling among them. One fell on the old lady in the pink dress and knocked her to the ground as she cried and screamed for help.

Outside, as the firefighters arrived on the scene, they were met by a group of masked young men. They came with bats, clubs, signs, and faces painted with swastikas, brass knuckles, and—most importantly—guns. When the firefighters yelled at them to move, to get out of the way, the men started to shoot.

They had come to hurt people, and they did.

CHAPTER 3

𐤀𐤍𐤆𐤁𐤈𐤎𐤏𐤑

She was the only survivor. The strange girl with the freakish appearance. As the firefighters and paramedics were finally able to get into the building, after the attackers had run and it had burned completely to the ground, they found her, still in her mother's arms, held tightly against her body. Her mother had tried to cover her face with a scarf, maybe to keep her from breathing smoke, and the media later speculated that maybe that had saved her life. There really wasn't any other explanation for how such a young baby could survive such a thing. It was either that or believe it was a miracle, but people liked the scarf explanation better. It made more sense. The pictures of the blackened mother, holding her infant, saving her life from the flames went around the world faster than any viral pictures of any cat ever had.

And they all agreed. What had happened was an atrocity. It was an act of terrorism. Yet, the perpetrators were never apprehended, and rumors soon began to be murmured that the police weren't doing enough to investigate it because the victims were all black. The world didn't care because they were all people of color and, therefore, their lives of less value than others. Tensions rose, not only in New Orleans but soon it spread to other big cities where clashes between blacks and the police were getting more and more frequent. Riots in the streets became an everyday thing. They marched in what were supposed to be peaceful protests, but some took advantage and smashed store windows and stole, destroying it for all the others. It was a protest, people acting out in despair because they didn't know what else to do because they felt worth less than everyone else in society, the experts explained on TV. But all the world saw was young black boys running amok.

On top of it all, the NFL decided to replace all players who refused to stand during the National Anthem with other players who would, and those replaced players were banned completely from ever playing again.

Meanwhile, Jetta was left in the care of her grandmother, who, on a regular basis, did her banishing rituals to try and push out the demon from inside the young girl. She would sing and chant and burn incense along with strange smelling candles and leave crystals all over the house to purify the place. She would even try and force the girl to eat herbs that she spat out just as fast as they came into her mouth.

Jetta didn't seem to mind much. She grew older and stronger, even though it was still whispered as she walked the streets with her grandmother that she was a witch, a demon sent to curse them, and that the fire had happened because of her.

Being only six years old, Jetta didn't care much what people said and her grandmother decided she couldn't hide her forever. The girl needed fresh air from time to time.

"So, let them talk," she finally concluded.

The old grandmother was becoming quite smitten with the little girl and cared deeply for her, even though she still believed she was sent from the evil spirits to curse them all. The way the world was going these days, it wouldn't matter much anyway. It could hardly get much worse, now could it?

Then the president was shot.

PART 1

CHAPTER 4

As soon as they found out the assassin had been black, things went from bad to worse for people of color. They weren't allowed to go to white schools anymore and couldn't even shop in same shops as whites without being harassed. Daily attacks on black neighborhoods followed. People were killed in the streets by masked men with swastikas on their sleeves, some beaten to death with clubs, others shot in front of their own houses. Even young children were killed for simply being of the same race as the man who had shot the president.

The assassin, it turned out, was part of an underground movement of people fighting for black separatism, called Black Liberty. Their goal was to be separated from the whites and, soon, that was exactly what happened.

It became *them or us* and you had to choose a side. There was nothing in between. People in mixed marriages were attacked in their homes and separated, husbands or wives killed in front of their loved ones.

Those that didn't split up were brutally killed in the streets, some even hung from the lampposts as a warning to others. And you couldn't hide. Your neighbor became your enemy.

It didn't take many years for the situation to accelerate into a state where it could be called a civil war. And that was exactly what they would later call it, *the Second Civil War*.

From the ashes of the old government rose a new leader who had new plans for the country. This leader, with a background as a general in the Air Force, and part of what they called the alt-right movement, was the one who had the vision of a different country, and a way to end the fighting, a way to stop the savagery.

It happened overnight. The first city to build a wall around itself was Boston. One morning, the citizens woke up to the military in the streets, setting up barbed wire and checkpoints all around the town. The point was to keep an eye on who came in and keep the fighting outside of town, was the explanation. And it worked. In the coming months, a calmness fell upon the city, as anyone fighting was simply thrown out and not let back in. The idea later spread to other cities. New York City was the next to follow, then Washington, D.C., LA, San Francisco, Miami, Savannah, and soon most of the bigger cities in the U.S. became protected areas where the citizens were safe from the fighting. Brick walls were later built where the barbed wire had been.

But that wasn't enough for self-acclaimed white president Patricia Neuman, who would later be called nothing

Part 1

but *Mother*, as she saw herself as the mother of a new and greater nation. Next, she started to throw out anyone of color from the cities she controlled. The military came at night and fetched them from their homes, deporting them to ghettos outside the towns. And not only blacks. Anyone of color was soon labeled as black too. That's what they called them. There was no African American anymore, no Asian, no Native American, and no more Hispanic or Middle Eastern people. If you weren't white, you were black. It was as simple as that.

Tired of the politically correct labels, the president—or Mother—simply put them all in one category. She started to talk about having dirt in your genes as opposed to being white and clean.

They might have thought it was wrong. Lots of them did. But none of the whites disputed this new approach once they found out what was really going on. After all, it was *them* who had killed the former president. *They* had started it all. *They* had been destroying this great nation for too long, as the new president told them. Every problem in this country was somehow related to people of color, to blacks.

"We are already divided. It's time we split up. To save this great nation of ours," she said, standing in the ruins of the White House, where she and her forces had set up headquarters.

At thirteen years old, Jetta watched the—later to be famous—speech on TV in her grandmother's small apartment in the French Quarter of New Orleans. When she turned off the TV, she heard the sound of heavy boots on the stairwell outside. Sounding like the drums from hell. Doors in the building were knocked in, people were screaming, shots were fired.

Jetta looked up at her grandmother, who stared at the front door, eyes wide, a breath stuck in her throat, her nails digging deep into the armrest of her old recliner.

"Nanna?"

CHAPTER 5

𐤀𐤍𐤆𐤁𐤏𐤙𐤕

They didn't give them time to pack their things. Still, Jetta managed to grab her old teddy bear and a ring her grandmother had given her that she said belonged to her mother before the soldiers grabbed her by the arm and carried her out of the apartment that had, up until now, been the home of her childhood. The soldiers carried her down the stairs, while she heard her grandmother crying and screaming behind her.

"Nanna!" Jetta cried, but she couldn't see her.

Jetta was placed on the ground outside, where an officer approached her and looked at her face, placing a hand underneath her chin to lift her face to better look at it.

"What do we do about this one, sir?" the soldier who had carried her, said.

The officer scrutinized Jetta's face, while Jetta watched her grandmother be put on a bus, a soldier pushing her forcefully.

"What are you, child?" the officer asked.

Jetta looked at him. She didn't answer because she didn't understand the question.

"Answer me, child. What are you?"

She shook her head, and then looked at the entrance to the bus, where she could no longer see her grandmother. Panic started to erupt, and Jetta's small body was shaking.

The officer grabbed her face and forced her to look at him. "What are you, child? Black or white?"

"I...I don't know."

The officer shook his head. "I've never seen one like this," he said to the soldier.

"Me either, sir."

"One side is pure as snow, yet the other is dirty."

"Clearly dirty, sir."

"Yeah. She's got dirt in her blood. You know the instructions, soldier. Anyone with any hint of *dirt* in their blood goes."

"Yes, sir."

The soldier saluted the officer, then grabbed Jetta by the arm and pulled her forcefully. He lifted her into the air and she began to cry. He walked to the bus and put her on the steps.

"This one goes too," he said addressed to the driver.

Jetta ran up the stairs, her eyes searching for her grandmother in the crowd, but she couldn't see her anywhere. People were standing so close, it was hard to breathe, and as more people were stuffed inside the bus,

Part 1

Jetta could no longer move. She was pinned between a seat and someone's belly, fighting to even breathe.

"Nanna?" she cried, but no one could hear her.

So many were screaming, whimpering, and crying out names of their loved ones, her voice was drowned out. The pushing and shoving got worse and as the bus took off, some guy in big black shoes trampled on Jetta.

CHAPTER 6

The ghetto was like a small city itself. Once Jetta managed to get herself off the bus, she saw barbed wire, tons of soldiers, and hundreds, maybe even thousands, of black people. All the faces were strained and the eyes filled with the terror of uncertainty.

They were ordered to place all their belongings in a pile, including any electronics and cellphones since they wouldn't be able to use any of them in the ghetto. They would get it all back later, the soldiers said. But no one understood how they would ever be able to tell the belongings apart and get them to the right people when they were all put in the same pile. Those that complained, or even asked about it, were beaten with batons or tased.

They told them to get into lines and to walk forward. Jetta called her grandmother's name but received no answer. She pulled the shirt of someone walking next to her, but he pushed her away, mumbling something about

Part 1

her being a Halfling, and belonging to them, not belonging here.

Jetta didn't understand.

"Excuse me? Have you seen my grandmother?" she asked a lady walking behind her.

"Don't talk to me, you disgusting creature," the woman replied, then pulled her child away from her.

That was when Jetta realized that her grandmother had been protecting her. She had kept her at home and homeschooled her and told her to never go out alone, only so Jetta didn't have to face people and how they felt about her. She was used to staring eyes but had never realized people would find her appalling.

She looked at her own reflection in a car parked on the side of the road. Jetta stopped to glance at it, and for the first time, she found herself hating what she saw. She touched her face on both sides and realized she liked neither of the sides anymore. They were both ugly. Then she pulled the hoodie of her shirt to cover her face, so no one would see it.

A soldier came running to her, hit her in the face with his rifle, then yelled at her to keep moving.

"Don't stop; keep moving," he yelled first at her, then at everyone else. "You need to keep the line moving."

Jetta wiped the blood off her nose, pulled the hoodie further up, to make sure it covered her face completely, then hurried back into the line, remembering her neighbor, John, who had been on the police force before this all had started. He had told her how he had been stripped of his badge one day, just out of the blue. One day, when arriving at work, he'd been called into the chief's office and told to hand over his badge and gun, told that he was no longer a part of the force.

"No explanation. No reason. No nothin'. Just like that, they took away everything from me," he told Jetta's grandmother, sitting in the kitchen of their apartment.

He told her there used to be blacks in both the police force and the Army, but not anymore. Blacks were not even allowed to be firefighters anymore. They were all replaced with smart robots, he said. But the robots were created to all look like white people.

"They're getting rid of us," he said, looking at Jetta as he spoke. "I'm telling ya. It's comin'."

Jetta's grandmother had called it nonsense, but Jetta had sensed something in her voice that made her know she wasn't so convinced. Just a few days earlier, she had been discussing it with another of their neighbors, Miss Melissa, who used to be a schoolteacher but wasn't allowed to teach white kids anymore, according to the new regulations.

"There are rumors," Melissa had said. "Of trains. Black freight trains that they use to transport people of color off to secret camps, moving across the country, the white man's sins covered by the blackness of the night."

Again, Jetta's grandmother had answered with a scoff. "Nothing but rumors and fairytales, Melissa. Nothing but fairy tales. You believe in Little Red Riding Hood too?"

And then they had laughed. But it wasn't a happy laughter.

CHAPTER 7

She was put inside an apartment with six other people she didn't know. There was only one bedroom and only one bed for all of them to share. Jetta slept on the floor, along with a few others. Weeks went by, and those weeks turned into months. She didn't know any of the others and kept to herself, keeping her face covered by the hoodie. Mostly, she sat in the corner, her teddy bear in hand, looking out the small window, down into the courtyard where people walked around like caged animals.

The buildings were all new, made especially for them, they were told. Yet there was no clean running water and no air-conditioning, which made the place very warm, especially with the summer approaching. Food was distributed once a day when a big truck brought it inside the fence, and it was thrown out to the crowd. There were days when Jetta didn't get anything at all to eat because she was too short to catch it, or someone pulled it from her hands if she did.

Four of the people she lived with were all part of the same family. A mom and dad and two teenagers. They stuck together, keeping the rest out, hoarding the one bed. The others were an elderly woman, who had been badly beaten on her way to the ghetto, and a young boy, who—like Jetta—sat in a corner and stared into thin air most of the time. Every now and then, Jetta saw a tear escape his eye and roll across his cheek.

One day, she went to his corner and sat down next to him.

"Hi, I'm Jetta," she said. "What's your name?"

The boy's big eyes landed on her as he searched for her eyes inside the hoodie. Jetta smiled, then pulled it back a little. When the boy saw her face, he started to scream. He held both his hands to his face and cried out so loudly everyone in the small one-bedroom apartment stopped to look at them.

"Monster! Monster!"

The two adults approached Jetta and pulled the hoodie all the way off. The mother gasped and drew back, the dad right behind her.

"Dear Lord," he said, scrutinizing her. "What are you?"

"She's a freak," the mother said.

"You're half white," the dad said. "You're one of them, aren't you? Were you sent here to be a spy? Were you? To tell on us, give them a reason to kill us, huh? I told you this would happen. Over and over again, I said it, didn't I? All they're waiting for is for us to make one mistake, one wrong move, and then, they'll strike. Kill us all. Is that

Part 1

why you're here, huh? Of course, they would use a child. Nothing but pure evil."

The dad leaned over Jetta and slapped her face. The slap stung across her cheek and she whimpered. He then spat on her and kicked her. The mother soon followed, throwing in a kick herself, and soon the two teenagers were doing it too. They slapped Jetta and kicked her in the stomach. Jetta whimpered and curled up into a ball, letting them beat her, thinking she deserved it, believing she deserved it all. It was, after all, her fault, wasn't it? She had heard it all her life. It was her fault her parents died in that fire, along with all the others. She had brought it upon them and on the rest of the people. It was all because of her. Because she was a curse sent to Earth from the evil spirits. To torture them, to doom them all. She knew it was so, and so she let them beat her, thinking maybe they could beat all this evilness out of her, so she—and the world—could be set free.

CHAPTER 8

The beating was bad, but still, Jetta woke up the next morning with no signs of being hurt, except for a few bruises on her legs that disappeared after a few hours. As the sun rose and shone into the small warm apartment, rapidly heating up the corner where she lay curled up, Jetta realized the bruises were all gone. Not even were her eyes swollen or her cheeks red.

The mother was the first to notice as she got out of bed.

"What the...? Sam? Sam, come look at this!"

The dad did, and he too had to look again a few times before believing his own eyes.

"How is that even...possible?"

They both backed up—their eyes torn in fear—as the dad repeated his question from the night before.

"What *are* you?"

Jetta looked terrified, yet fascinated at her arms and legs, distinctively remembering hearing her arm break as the teenage son stepped on it the night before. She lifted it into the air and looked at it, turning it in the sparse sunlight. Not a scratch.

"This isn't natural," the mother said, her voice shaking. "The way she looked last night...I thought she would be dead by now, but...this?"

The older teenage children approached Jetta, staring at her with big glaring eyes. The mother grabbed them both and pulled them away.

"Don't go too close to it." Then she turned to her husband and, even though she spoke with a low voice, Jetta still heard it perfectly.

"What do we do about her?"

"I don't know," Sam replied.

"We can't have her here. I can't stand the thought of her here...with us. I won't be able to sleep. I can't stand it, Sam. I just can't."

"I know. I know."

They glanced at Jetta once again, then looked away.

"Can we kill her?" the woman asked, lowering her voice to almost a whisper.

"One less mouth to feed," Sam said. "I say no one will miss her. There are way too many people in this place anyway. And there is barely enough food for everyone as it is. People are getting desperate around here. Hunger does that to people. No one would notice."

"I heard they have some sickness in the building next door. Three people died in there yesterday," she said.

"Maybe we could take her over there and let nature take care of her," Sam said. "Take the old lady with her.

She doesn't have long either. That just leaves us with the boy. He doesn't eat much, though."

The woman sighed. She looked at her husband, and then put a hand to cover her mouth like she had just realized something.

"Oh, no, Sam."

Sam nodded and rubbed his forehead. "I can't believe I just said those things. What has become of us?"

"It's the hunger," the woman said. "And this damn place. The walls, I can't stand being locked in like this. Will we ever get out of here?"

Sam turned around and looked at the corner where Jetta had been sitting. "She's gone," he said. "Guess the problem solved itself."

Jetta, who had heard the entire conversation, had snuck out of the apartment, teddy bear in her hand, and was running down the stairs of the fifteen-story building, doing what she should have done when she first got to this strange place months earlier but had been too afraid.

Search for her grandmother.

CHAPTER 9

The ghetto was enormous for such a small girl. It was like a city sealed from the outside world by an eleven-foot-tall wall with barbed wire on top, and guards by the only entrance leading outside. Jetta searched the entire building she had been in for the past several months first but found nothing but despair and fear-torn eyes in dark bony faces.

Jetta walked through apartment after apartment, knocking on doors, asking, pleading for news about her old grandmother.

"If she's old, she probably died," a tall man said and slammed the door in her face.

She kept her face hidden the best she could and only peeked out using her one brown eye, hiding the side of her that people here loathed.

"I'm looking for my grandmother," she said after knocking on the next door. The woman who opened it shook her head. "We have no old people here. Try the courtyard. Many people are sleeping outside because there is not enough room."

Jetta nodded and walked on, knocking on several other doors on her way, but getting nothing but shaking heads. A few let her go inside and search, and what she found was forever burned into her memory. Everywhere she went, she saw nothing but misery. People were dying in every corner, thin skeleton-looking people, old people, young people, people who were weak or sick. Some reached out for her, asking her for food or water, their skinny arms pulling her clothes.

"How do you expect your grandmother to be alive?" someone asked her when she ran into the courtyard and started to call her name.

The guy was tall and muscular, wearing a dirty tank top not covering many of his tattoos and baggy pants. Could have been what her grandmother would have called a gang member once, when they still could walk the streets and would see them on corners. Or a drug dealer. The type she would tell her to stay far away from. He was young, maybe four or five years older than Jetta.

"There is nothing but disease inside those buildings," he continued. "Soon, they will all be dead. It has started. They're getting rid of us." He nodded toward the guards at the entrance. Soldiers marched outside in the streets, making sure no one tried to escape. Jetta had seen more than a dozen try. They were all shot dead. No one got out.

"They knew it would happen. When you put this many people in a small area with no AC or proper

Part 1

plumbing, diseases start to spread. They're gonna leave us here to die. I stay out here," he said. "You should too. The old will go first, then the children."

Jetta looked up at the guy. He nodded towards another group of bigger guys at the other end of the courtyard. There wasn't much sunlight let inside the yard from the tall buildings and walls surrounding it.

"Those guys control the food. They're the strongest here and take first. I stay close to them to make sure I get enough. You should too. If you want to survive, that is."

Jetta nodded and bit her lip. She didn't really feel as weak or famished as the rest of them, but she was hungry. She wondered about her grandmother and looked up at the tall building in front of them. Someone had told her there were about forty more of them just like that one. It had taken her all day to do just one. It would take more than a month to search the entire ghetto. And, by then, it might be too late.

Jetta put her back up against the wall of the building and slid to the ground, pulling her legs close, resting her chin on her knees.

The guy was about to leave, when he hesitated, biting his lip. He shifted his weight a few times like he was making a big decision, then approached her again.

"I'm Tyler, by the way."

He reached out his hand. Jetta took it, using her black hand, making sure she only looked at him sideways.

"I'm Jetta."

"Little J," he said with half a smile. "Nice to meet you."

He sank down next to her on the hard concrete ground. He looked towards the wall.

"I used to have my own shop inside the town walls. Cars."

He looked at his hands and turned them in the light. "I could fix anything with these. It was a dream of mine, since childhood. To have my own shop. At fifteen, I was thrown out of my school because of the new rules of segregation. I didn't believe they were bad. Just fearful, I told my mother. I serviced so many of *them* in my shop. Guess it kept me alive. I helped them with all their problems, big or small, finding pleasure in helping them. My mom used to tell me I was their slave. Soon, they would call me *boy*, she said. 'You're nothing but a nigger serving his master,' she would say. 'They don't care about you. To them, you're just another black kid looking for trouble.' And it would hurt me so bad when she said stuff like that, you know? 'Cause I was proud of myself. I had built a business. I kept my family alive and protected this way. And I made money. Not much, but enough to eat, you know? I thought I was just like them, that we could be equal. They came to me for help. Me. But then, one day, I was out driving and I was pulled over. They took me down, beat me half to death, and made me realize I wasn't. Knocked me right back where I belonged. I was nothing in their eyes. Just another black boy. That was when I knew. One day, they would come for us. One day, they would decide to just get rid of us all. It all started when they came to my shop and closed it down. They took it from me, handing me a letter telling me it now

Part 1

belonged to the government. I didn't even know they could do that. Guess I was the fool there, huh? A week or so later, I ended up here. My mom caught a fever and died three days ago and now I'm alone. I should have left while I could. Should have gone with my brother. I stayed to protect my mother, who couldn't travel. Meanwhile, my brother is out there fighting. He and his buddies escaped before they came for us. Joined Black Liberty's armed forces. I heard they bombed the subway in New York recently. Someone in building 4D told me."

Jetta looked up at Tyler. "How's that supposed to help?"

Tyler chuckled. "You're just a kid. You stick with Tyler and he will help you survive. You stick with Tyler, you hear, Little J?"

So, she did. After all, he was the first person there to actually want her to stick around. Covering the blonde side of her face and keeping her left hand inside the shirt, so he wouldn't see the white skin, she stayed right there by his side, ate what he brought her, what he fought the crowd to get, slept leaning against his shoulder, and listened to his stories all day long, making time go faster as people fell like flies around them.

CHAPTER 10

"I THINK I may have found a way out."

Tyler sat down next to Jetta. He was sweating heavily and wiped his forehead with the back of his hand. He had been gone for an hour or so, like he usually was around noon. Jetta didn't know what he did, but she often saw him walking around among people, talking to them, and sometimes he would come back with a package of cigarettes or maybe even—and that was *very* rare—a candy cane for her.

She never asked questions, just took it and enjoyed it.

Tyler was speaking with nothing but a whisper, looking anxiously around him.

"You listen closely to me, Little J. There's a lady," he said, breathing heavily. He paused.

A group of women walked past them. The courtyard had become more and more crowded since people had realized they were getting sick from staying inside with all the diseased people. Just breathing the air in there could kill you.

Tyler waited till they had passed before he continued:

"A white one. She comes here once a week. She's an undertaker and helps remove the dead ones. She has been known to help some folks get out. But you gotta be well. She'll check you for symptoms. You don't have any, do ya?"

Jetta thought about what symptoms were and what they looked like, then shook her head. She had never been sick a day in her life.

"No throwing up?"

She shook her head again.

"Rashes?"

"No."

"Headaches?"

"No."

Jetta realized she didn't even know what a headache was. She had felt the pain when Sam and his family had beaten her, but that didn't last long. Other than that, she didn't remember ever feeling pain.

"Now, me, I never get sick," Tyler said. "I'm as strong as an ox. Let me feel your forehead."

Before she could react, Tyler had reached inside her hoodie.

Jetta pulled back and, as she did, the hoodie slipped and revealed a little of the white part of her face. Jetta pulled it back in place as quickly as she could, hoping Tyler didn't see it.

Tyler paused and removed his hand. He stared at her for a very long time, not saying a word, and she felt anxious.

Would he tell on her? If people knew, they might want to kill her for being half white.

Tyler bit his lip like he was thinking very thoroughly about something.

"Nah, you're probably fine." He handed her a piece of bread. "Here. Eat. You have to be strong. The lady comes tomorrow, and I've put a word in for us with the people that arrange who goes. I think we might have a chance. Especially since you're a child. Now, I'm eighteen, so I can't go for being a child no more, but you can. How old are ya?"

"Fourteen," Jetta said, remembering she had spent her birthday in the apartment with a bunch of people she didn't know, not telling anyone.

"Well, you're small. You could easily be eleven. Or ten. If she asks, then that's what you are, all right? They mostly take the children. But you've gotta say you need me with you, you hear me? I've been good to you, now it's your turn to pay me back. Tell them I'm your brother."

"But what about my grandmother?"

Tyler sighed and ate some bread too. "I told ya, kid. She's probably dead by now. Old folks go first. Now, eat."

CHAPTER 11

Tyler held Jetta's hand tightly in his as he led her into the building where they were going to meet the woman. Tyler had pulled her hoodie tight again and again as they crossed the courtyard and she had noticed his hands were shaking. Two men bigger than Tyler approached them as soon as they were inside.

"This is the girl," he said.

Jetta looked down at her feet like Tyler had told her to, making sure her face was fully covered. Tyler handed them a small bundle. Jetta looked up just enough to see it shift hands.

"It's all there. Enough for the both of us."

One of the men nodded. "Follow me," he said.

Tyler pulled Jetta's hand and they followed the man inside an apartment where someone who looked like a space man to Jetta was bent over the body of an old man in a bed.

A voice from inside the space suit said to the man

next to her, while shaking her head, "This one is dead too."

The space suit then turned, and Jetta now saw a face behind the glass. The face of a white woman. She looked tired, torn, and hurt. When she saw Jetta, she smiled. She had a nice smile.

"A child. How wonderful," she said.

She knelt in front of Jetta, who only looked at her by turning her black side toward her.

"We will have to get you out of here," she said. "I told them to bring me all the children they could find that weren't sick. You aren't sick, are you?"

"She's not," Tyler said.

The lady looked at Jetta, scrutinizing her. "I need to check you myself."

"I already checked her," Tyler said. "She's fine."

"Let me just..." she brought out a thermometer. "I need to get this in your mouth, sweetie," she said and reached it inside the hoodie.

Jetta recoiled.

"She's a little shy," Tyler said. "Scared."

"Don't be afraid, sweetheart. I'm not gonna hurt you. I'm just gonna put this thing in your mouth real quick and get your temperature..." The lady reached the stick inside. "Just open your mouth for me."

Jetta opened the one side and let the stick in under her tongue. It beeped and the lady looked happy.

"No fever. That's good. That's really good. Now, can you stick out your tongue for me?"

Jetta shook her head.

Part 1

"She's been through a lot," Tyler said.

Jetta could hear he was nervous.

The lady sighed. "I just need to make sure she's not sick. I can get some antibiotics but not enough for everyone I bring out. It will raise suspicions. I'm risking my life doing this. Anyone who helps your kind is executed. I have to check her for a rash too on her back and stomach. The lady looked at Jetta. "Would you let me do that? Otherwise, I will have to take someone else. I can only take two today. The inspections are getting stricter. There are other children waiting. I can take you two if you let me check the both of you. But she's got to let me. Otherwise, your spot goes to someone else. I am sorry, but those are the rules."

Tyler nudged Jetta and she finally turned her face to look at the woman. The lady froze as she looked inside the hoodie.

"Dan?" she said to the man in a space suit behind her, her voice shivering slightly.

"Ma'am?"

"Could you leave for a second? This girl needs a little privacy."

"Sure."

The white man left and the lady looked at Jetta. She lifted her shirt and looked at her stomach and back, gently touching the stripe going down the middle of her body. She sighed and let the shirt come back down.

"I see no rash. I can take her. And you with her," she said addressed to Tyler. "But how do you expect a girl like that to survive in a world like this? If one side won't kill her, the other will." She pointed a finger at Tyler. "I'll get her out of here and to a safe place. But you never leave her side, you hear me? You promise me that? I am not taking you if you don't make me that promise. You're not just using her to get out of here, you hear me? You stay by her side *no matter what.*"

Tyler nodded. "All right. All right."

CHAPTER 12

THEY HAD to wait for two hours inside the apartment, along with several dead bodies. Jetta pulled her knees up against her chin and hugged her legs, rocking back and forth and looking down.

Tyler coughed. "That smell!"

Jetta looked up at him, then sniffed the air. "I don't smell anything," she said.

He scoffed. "You're kidding me, right? You're telling me you can't smell the stench of decay? My eyes are literally watering."

Jetta thought it smelled good and felt embarrassed, so she didn't tell him. To her, it smelled like it had just rained. She liked it.

"There is something seriously wrong with you if you can't smell that," Tyler said and pinched his nose. He looked at her with a wry smile. "But, I guess we've already established that, haven't we?" He poked her teasingly and she laughed. "You're a little weirdo, aren't you?"

It felt good to laugh again. Jetta couldn't remember when she had laughed the last time.

The door opened and the two white people entered in their yellow space suits, carrying another stretcher.

"This is the last one...for today," the lady said and put the stretcher down. Then they left again.

Jetta stared at the body on the stretcher, then let out a small sound that might have sounded like a whimper.

"What?" Tyler asked.

Jetta rose to her feet, forgetting everything around her, and stormed to the stretcher, yelling out:

"Nanna!"

Tyler was right behind her. "Little J!"

Jetta threw herself on top of her grandmother, clinging to her dead body as Tyler grabbed her and pulled her away.

"Nanna! Tyler, that's my Nanna," she said, agitated and strangely excited, staring at him with both eyes. She knew she was supposed to feel something, a sadness, or even hopelessness, but she didn't.

"I know," he said. "I know."

Jetta stared at her grandmother with deep fascination, as only seeing a dead person could make her stare. Tyler misunderstood her and thought she was about to cry. He grabbed her, wrapping himself around her. He held her close and rocked her for a few minutes while the two white people came back, carrying coffins inside the room.

"Is everything all right?" the lady asked when she spotted Tyler and Jetta in a close embrace.

Part 1

Tyler nodded. "We're fine," he said.

Jetta knew he was lying. She could hear his heartbeat through his shirt and instantly she knew he was scared that the white people wouldn't take them if Jetta acted out. He needed her to be calm and collected. How were they going to go through a checkpoint if she could be heard crying? The white people wouldn't take such a risk. He had to shut her up, to make her stop crying.

But how could she tell him she didn't feel any need to cry? What she did need was to get out of this place just as much as he did. She looked at him and smiled. Tyler's heartbeat came down and he relaxed.

"Good girl. Good girl."

The lady approached them and spoke to Jetta. "Here, sweetheart, you're going in this one."

She grabbed Jetta's hand in hers and guided her to a big white coffin where they both looked inside.

"There's a false bottom," the white lady said. "You'll be underneath and this old lady on top. All you have to promise me is to be very quiet, okay? Don't make a sound or the guards might hear you. This is very important. Not a single sound. No giggling and no crying. Do you understand? These guards are not human. They might look like it, but they're not. They're cleverly engineered robots and they have ten times the hearing we humans have."

Jetta watched while they prepared the coffin for her. She looked at her grandmother, who was lying on the worn-out stretcher next to the coffin, remembering the many hours they used to play cards at the apartment back home. How they used to laugh together. For some reason, she began to think about how her grandmother would teach her about the spirits and gods, how to make sure not to anger them, how to please them and make sure they would give you success in life. And, more than anything, she taught her how to be careful of the god of storms, to not anger him, and always make sure you had food for him to eat.

"Okra," she would say. "Always have okra in the house for him." For that reason, Nanna always had an entire cabinet full of okra, just in case.

Jetta found the memory enchanting and wondered if her Nanna was with her gods right now.

CHAPTER 13

It was dark inside the coffin. Dark and hot as the minivan with the five coffins in it bumped forward toward the checkpoint leading to the great outside. Jetta was sweating and she felt like she was being crushed. There was no room to move at all, and she knew she wasn't allowed to.

Jetta closed her eyes and pictured herself back at the apartment with her grandmother and not having her dead body on top of her, going towards what could be the death of her.

The van stopped and there were muffled voices outside.

You've got to be quiet. Just be quiet.

Jetta thought about her grandmother and wondered how she was supposed to go on, what would be on the other side of all this—*if* she made it out—when her grandmother wasn't there to take care of her. After her parents died, her grandmother had always been there. Always.

The voices outside grew louder and it sounded like a door was opened. Jetta held her breath as she heard the voices come closer and someone climb inside the back of the van. There was someone there.

A robot soldier. It'll hear me. It'll hear my heartbeat. Or it will hear Tyler and then me.

Jetta felt like crying. The last thing she wanted was to go back to that place. She would rather die than go back.

"Can you lift the lid off that one?" the soldier said. If he was, in fact, a robot, he sounded exactly like a human, but Jetta had heard they did that...that people couldn't tell the difference anymore. It was what had given the whites the big advantage in the war.

"That one? Why?"

Jetta recognized the voice of the white lady. She sounded upset, agitated even. Jetta was certain she could hear the woman's ragged breathing. Could the soldiers hear it too? Could they hear how scared she was?

"Just do it."

"You're the one risking getting infected," the lady said.

"I'll take that risk," the soldier said.

Of course, you will. You're a robot. Robots can't get sick.

There was the sound of a lid being opened. It wasn't Jetta's. Soon, the lid was closed again.

"Okay," the soldier said.

Jetta could hear him outside her coffin now.

"Now, that one," the soldier said.

Jetta held her breath once again.

"Now! I don't have all day."

Part 1

Jetta closed her eyes when she felt a hand touch her face. She opened her eyes and looked up. Her grandmother's hand had fallen into the crack between the false bottom and the wall of the coffin. Jetta clasped her mouth as the lid to the coffin was opened. She lay as quiet as humanly possible, her grandmother's hand in her face, terrified the soldier would hear her rapid heartbeat.

It took forever and Jetta could hardly hold her breath any longer; still, she knew if she did breathe, they would definitely hear her. A dog suddenly barked and someone yelled from the outside, distracting the soldier.

"We have a runner!"

"Shoot," the soldier said.

Breathing freely again, Jetta heard the sound of him jumping out of the van and what sounded like hundreds of boots following him. Then came the sound of shots being fired, and then the eerie quietness before someone screamed from inside the ghetto. Jetta knew the procedure of sounds a little too well. She had seen it one too many times. Sometimes, she would even see the person who had been shot's relatives run out through the checkpoint after him, only to get shot themselves as well.

The lid to the coffin was meanwhile closed and the minivan hurried off.

When Jetta finally dared to open her eyes again, she stared straight into those of her grandmother.

CHAPTER 14

"Nanna?"

Jetta said it a little too loud. Luckily, the van was bumping forward so no one heard. Her grandmother's eyes kept staring at her from above. Jetta couldn't breathe.

"But...but you are..."

Her grandmother didn't say anything. She smelled like the rain. Jetta realized her grandmother's body hadn't moved. Her body was still lying on the false bottom, on top of her in the exact same position as earlier. It was only her head that had turned all the way around on her neck and now her eyes looked through the crack between the false bottom and the side of the coffin, where her hand had fallen down previously.

Had it stroked Jetta's cheek after all?

Jetta couldn't see all of her grandmother's face, mostly her eyes as they stared at her. She could also see her lips as they turned upwards into a grin. Her grey and steely lips.

Part 1

"How?"

The rational part of Jetta told her it was just a dream, or some hallucination created by her mind caused by the trauma of seeing her grandmother, her only relative left, dead in the apartment back at the ghetto. That same part insisted that if she closed her eyes or even blinked, the illusion would go away and her grandmother would be lost again forever. So, she didn't. She kept her eyes wide open and stared into her grandmother's for as long as she could, remembering all the days and nights she had spent with her as a child, missing hearing her voice.

But there was also another part of her, a deeply hidden part, that knew that this *was* her grandmother now, this was the shape she was in now. She was actually there, dead. Yet still somehow looking at her granddaughter from the world of the spirits.

"But..."

She had so many questions, so much she wanted to ask her dear grandmother, but her grandmother couldn't speak, and soon the van came to a halt. Jetta held her breath and waited. She listened while her small grandmother's eyes were still looking at her from above. They were staring, not blinking once.

Voices on the outside, the sound of loud agitated talking. Jetta closed her eyes in anxiety.

Another checkpoint.

Voices kept going for a few minutes before the back door to the van opened. A voice spoke, another answered, but only muffled sounds reached Jetta. Then, the sound of the door closing again, followed shortly by the wondrous sound of the engine roaring as the van took off once again.

Jetta breathed and opened her eyes, only to find that her grandmother's eyes were no longer staring back her. Her body, head, and hand were all back in place on top of Jetta as she had been when they left.

CHAPTER 15

The van finally stopped and Jetta felt the coffin being carried somewhere, then there was silence. For a very long time. Nothing but darkness and silence. There came a point when she considered knocking on the sides, but she didn't dare to.

Finally—hours later—the lid was opened and light shone into the coffin. They lifted her grandmother off and opened the false bottom. Jetta held a hand to cover her eyes from the bright light. It was coming from a light bulb under the ceiling above her.

"Sorry for the long wait," the woman said as Jetta sat up.

They were both there. The white man and the white woman, now without their spacesuits. They were smiling compassionately at Jetta.

"We had to wait till the sun had set upon the city," the man said. "To make sure no one noticed."

"I'm in the city again?" she asked.

"Yes. New Orleans. We brought you to our house. Inside the walls. Both of you. There is nowhere else for you to go. Outside, on the other side of the walls, is nothing but death. Especially for someone like you. No one is out there anymore except soldiers and criminals waiting to kill you for scraps. On the other side of the ghettos, it's nothing but wasteland and war. People fighting everywhere, burning down entire cities. There are no laws, no one to help you if you're unarmed. It's no place for someone like you. Most of the children I have helped, I took to an orphanage outside of town, but unfortunately, that was burned down a few days ago. I don't even know if anyone survived."

Tyler came up behind her. "But in here, we'll be killed if they find us. This is white man's city."

The white woman nodded. "I know. But you'll be safe here. We'll make sure you stay safe."

Tyler looked at the man, then back at the woman. "But if we're found, they will kill you as well."

They looked at each other. "We know," the man said. "We know."

"But we can't just do nothing, can we?" the lady said. "After all, the world will not be destroyed by those who do evil, but by those who watch them without doing anything."

"Albert Einstein," Tyler said.

The man smiled and reached out his hand. "I'm Peter. Peter Johnson."

"I'm Joy," the woman said and waved a little awkwardly. "We have a son, Philip, here too, but he's

Part 1

asleep. Now, I'll take you to the attic. There's an entrance in the back. We run our undertaker business from this house, but no one ever uses the attic. The entrance is covered by a movable case of shelves with cans. It can only be pulled away from our side of it."

Joy showed them up the stairs through a small kitchen and into the pantry, where Peter grabbed the shelves and pulled them aside to expose a door behind it. He opened it and revealed a staircase.

"Here we go," he said. "Come on. You must hurry."

Jetta looked up into the darkness. Tyler was right behind her.

"I'll go first," he said.

Tyler disappeared up the stairwell, almost running. Jetta followed, taking first a few cautious steps upwards, then pausing while the door was closed behind her and the faces of Joy and Peter disappeared along with the light.

ORDER YOUR COPY TODAY!

GO HERE TO ORDER:

https://www.amazon.com/GIRL-DIVIDED-Willow-Rose-ebook/dp/B0778WX62V

Printed in Great Britain
by Amazon